THE PALE FOX

DAVID LEONARD
"THE GENERAL"

The Pale Fox

By David Leonard

Cover Created & Designed by Jazzy Kitty Publications

Logo Designs by Andre M. Saunders/Jess Zimmerman

Editor: Anelda L. Attaway

Co-Editor: David Leonard

AN INSTRUCTION FROM THE AUTHOR

If you are a Black male that was born in the year 2000, re-read the two quotes in my dedication by Frantz Fanon as many times as needed, and after you re-read them, ask yourself the questions, "Who am I?" and "What is my purpose as a Black man?" If you cannot answer those two questions, then you are ready to read this book.

David Leonard aka The General"

DEDICATION

This entire work is dedicated to Frantz Fanon, who gave me the answer.

"I came into the world imbued with the will to find meaning into things, my spirit filled with the desire to attain to the source of the world, and then I found that I was an object in the midst of other objects."

"I was indignant, and I demanded an explanation. Nothing happened. I burst apart, now the fragments have been put together again by another self."

Frantz Fanon Blackskin White Masks.

ACKNOWLEDGMENT

Inspiration can come in many various forms, I must state that mine came from God. My Acknowledgements would be endless because my Love is too great. Having a vision and pursuing it can be a lonely path.

I have much gratitude and love to JKP (Jazzy Kitty Publications) and my publisher Anelda Attaway. Also, to my typist, friend, and sister, Lawanda Jackson,

To my wife and children because they destroyed a lonely path of doubt and teaching me that you must do the thing you think you cannot do, by all means necessary.

I would like to let all readers understand that I wrote this book which would be considered fictional writing for non-fictional purposes, simply because fiction can be more interesting for the simple fact the author can tell the truth without humiliating him or herself. I fast and meditate that this book helps someone.

TABLE OF CONTENTS

TABLE OF CONTENTS

INTRODUCTION

I am not too proponent in writing long introductions. I am a fast-paced writer and very straight forward with any of my literary works. First and foremost, I must pay homage to Marimba Ani who I gained insight from concerning the title of her book titled, "Yorugu" which means Pale Fox. One must do their own investigation into the Dogon African religion to understand "The Pale Fox."

Many Black men are going to see themselves in many chapters within this novel and some will be in denial, and this is the same for Whites. The two main characters are 100% fictional, however, all mind-states that the main character Dru transforms into are all 100% non-fiction. The mind-states are my own life experiences and testimonies and observations that I received from other Black men. There are many Blacks that will probably be enraged that I took such serious matters that happen daily within the African American population and turned these matters into a mythological story (urban) and I am not surprised nor am I concerned. No one is ever-challenging urban novelists that write deadly literature that does nothing but keep Black men into a circular dimension.

This novel is geared to cause a thought disturbance in certain Black males, particularly Black young men, born in 2000 or later to take a clear look at themselves and the world around them.

CHAPTER 1

Part One – Ma'at – Judgement

"I give you everlasting life in your human experience!"

"But why?! I have fulfilled my duty."

"Yes, you have had many duties, but you did not fulfill and understand me! Therefore, she will find you, but you must have her call your name, and then you shall be allowed to die. The judgement is sealed."

CHAPTER 2

University of Illinois in Chicago, 2016

Penny, Tiffany, and Ebony sat in the student dining hall enjoying their lunch on an early morning in November. It was almost time for mid-terms, and the girls always hooked up as a think tank for every exam. They all were friends since high school and all inspiring anthropologists.

"Hey, Penny look! There's that guy you like," Tiffany said.

Unlike Tiffany and Ebony, Penny was a shy girl. Mulatto girl, plus sized, and 5'9", which was kind of tall for a girl.

"Well, you need to go talk to him before I do, cuz he is fine as Heaven," Ebony said.

"I wonder what his major is?" Penny asked while sipping her coffee.

"Umm that's why you need to get up off your scary shy ass and go talk to him," Tiffany said.

"Girl, I don't even have the time. Plus, look he got a cigarette behind his ear."

"Penny you're so full of it. Excuses, excuses. And just to make you mad, I'm a talk to him tomorrow just to see what his name is and you betta hope he ain't got no girlfriend," Ebony said.

"Okay, fine, if he comes tomorrow, I'll go talk to him. Damn you make me sick!"

Penny said as her dream guy that she had been watching since the beginning of the semester. Before he got to the door, he slowly turned to make eye contact.

"Oh gawd, he just caught me staring at him," Penny thought to herself.

His slight smile let her know he was watching the whole time.

"See girl, that's that come holla at me smile," Ebony said.

"Girl, shut up, I saw it," Penny said. But unfortunately, she might have waited too late.

- 3 -

CHAPTER 3

Five Days Later – 3:30 a.m.

Many thoughts ran through Penny's mind as she laid in her bed doing some late-night studying.

"I can't believe his ass never showed up again. I'm so pissed at his ass. If he were here right now, I'd ask him how he could just come in every day at the same time and just stop?" Penny stopped her crazy thoughts and laughed.

I'm definitely tripping, he probably don't like plus sized or mixed girls anyway.

Penny got up to roam through her student apartment that sat right across from campus. It was a Friday night and she would always stand looking through her patio doors. Penny giggled to herself as she looked over at the dorms at the kids drinking and partying because most college kids never closed their blinds.

"Damn, I'm glad I stopped partying early. I probably wouldn't have made it this far."

Penny was always a firm believer of the saying, "Be careful what you ask for."

She looked over at the Political Science Building, the mysterious guy she had a crush on appeared. Penny's eyes lit up and she began to blush for a moment.

"Oh Wow! There he is!"

Penny couldn't take her eyes off him. He sat at the top of a long staircase, smoking a cigarette.

"So, he does live on campus?"

Penny moved to the side just in case he looked towards the window so he wouldn't see her, but as she peeked to look at him again, he swiftly went back down the stairs into the Political Science Building. Penny sat for a moment, confused.

"Okay, now what the hell is he doing in the basement of the Poli Sci Building this late? Maybe he doesn't go here. Maybe he's a janitor or something?"

Penny hurried and went back to her room to call Ebony. Her heart pounded as she slipped out of her jeans and pounced on her bed. Ebony answered wide awake as if she knew Penny was going to call.

"What's up girl?" Ebony answered.

"Hey, this Pen."

"I know it's you, silly. So, what's up? Why you up so late?" Ebony asked.

"You know I'm a night owl, but you won't believe who I just saw," Penny said.

"Who?" Ebony asked while smacking on the pizza she was eating.

"That guy we see every morning."

"Oh, your future husband?" Ebony joked.

"You're silly! But guess where I saw him at?" Penny asked.

"How would I know? Where girl?" Ebony asked sarcastically.

"Going in the basement of the Political Science Building about 10 minutes ago!" Ebony paused for a moment then asked, "you sure the basement?"

Penny sighed with impatience, "Um, duh? No, the damn penthouse of the Political Science Building... yes, the damn basement!"

"Damn my bad girl. Well, he ain't a janitor or maintenance, we never see him in a uniform. That's weird. So, what you gon' do?"

"I don't know, but I just thought of something. Maybe he does work for maintenance and he changed out of his uniform and is getting ready to go or something. You think?"

"Well, put it this way, at least you know he's around and since he works nights, you should bring him some lunch or something, Ms. Scary."

CHAPTER 4

3 a.m.

Penny sat patiently in her window talking to Ebony.

"So, what did you leave him?" Ebony asked eagerly.

"Some coffee and Krispy Kreme's with a note," Penny said as she nibbled on her pinky nail.

"What did the note say?"

"I just put from Penny and my number; you think he'll call?"

"Of course, girl. All men love women that feed them. I wish I could stay on the phone but I gotta get up early and meet my mom for lunch. Make sure you text me and tell me what happened."

"Okay, love ya sis, bye."

It was 3:35 a.m. and Penny's mysterious guy didn't come out and have a cigarette. But something happened that Penny never thought of. Three bums happened to be walking by and spotted the box of donuts and coffee. One by one, the donuts disappeared as the three bums wiped the glaze from their mouths. Penny's mouth was wide open.

"I don't believe this shit. You gotta be kidding me."

Before they could grab the coffee, the mysterious guy came up the stairs while lighting his cigarette.

"Yes, it's about time his ass showed up. I hope he kicks their ass!"

Penny watch anxiously waiting for him to pick up the coffee but her smile quickly vanished. He quickly grabbed the coffee, stuck the note in his pocket, and slapped hands with the bums before leaving.

Penny's nostrils flared, *"Now he knew damn well those donuts were for him."*

Penny calmed down for a minute watching the bums as they walked away into the night.

"Stop being mad, he must be a stand-up guy. He didn't care about the donuts but at least he got my number now."

CHAPTER 5

Her Mystery Guy

Monday morning exhausted Penny and after a three-hour mid-term exam, all Penny could think about was her warm bed and a cup of hot chocolate. Penny raced from the Social Science Building trying to get out of the cold rain, but even cold rain didn't stop her from scrolling through her phone hoping to see a missed call or a love text from the mysterious guy she had a crush on. Her heart pounded to see a message.

"Damn, it's not him! Damn message is from my student email."

Attn: Penny Hampton - Student ID - 1001849

From: Professor J. Brooks

Subject: Final Examination Assignment

All Students are required to conduct a research project concerning the social development of African American males and how the external environment effects language, dress, beliefs dealing with race, sex, etc. All students are instructed to gain consent from an African American male between the ages of 18 and 30. All students will be graded based upon the amount of hours that is spent with the individual and observation notes. This is a Pass or Fail exam. Due Date: 5-10-2016.

P.S. - No African American males on campus can be used.

"Damn, I can't stand this man! He ain't even graded the damn mid-terms yet! And where in the hell am I gonna find someone to research?"

Penny stopped for a moment looking at her phone, realizing she was standing about 10 feet from the staircase that led to the basement of the P.S. Building. She stared at the staircase for a moment, twisting her sandy brown curly hair.

"Fuck this shit, I'm gonna see for myself!"

Penny was shy, but when her confidence kicked in shyness was out the door. When she got to the staircase, she looked to make sure nobody saw her go in the basement. She knew it would look odd for a student going in the basement of a college building, at least from the outside. The rain got colder, and the wind blew wet autumn leaves which Penny hated. As she got to the door, the latch had no lock, and she didn't hesitate to open it. Penny walked in slowly to find what she expected. The basement was wet, pipes were everywhere, and was furnished with huge water heaters which made it extremely warm.

There was no sign of her mystery guy and it looked like no one had been in that part of the building in years. There was definitely no janitorial or maintenance work done regularly. Penny didn't have the slightest idea why he would be there, and there he definitely was. Penny smelled a cigarette. Since she didn't smoke, she could smell one a mile away. A non-smoker is like a blood hound to a smoker. Penny noticed that there was a vent close to the ceiling about five feet wide. Once she saw where the smoke was coming from, her only choice was to climb the iron ladder that was attached to the wall that would lead her to the air vent.

"I don't believe I'm gonna climb this ladder. My big ass is definitely not in shape for this shit."

Penny climbed the iron ladder slowly and her mystery guy watched with a smirk on his face. He stood behind one of the water heaters watching Penny's hips move from left to right.

"Hmm, look at the ass and hips on her," he thought to himself.

Penny finally made it to the top and the ledge was only two feet wide. Penny kneeled down to see inside the vent. She sighed and took a deep breath. She was amazed to see on the other side of the well there was a

10x10 space with a small television, homemade carpet, sleeping bad, and four Army duffle bags.

"Oh-My-God," Penny thought, covering her mouth.

She saw the cigarette burning and her note next to an ashtray. She could tell he was near because he even had a MacBook that was still on. Penny bent over on her knees trying to see if he was anywhere to be seen when suddenly she felt a gentle poke on her ass from his finger.

"You're a lousy cat burglar," Penny's mystery guy said.

Penny jumped nearly falling but he grabbed her waist and sat her down on the ledge. Penny stared at the young brown skinned man that she saw every morning in the dining hall; she was speechless.

"You should have told me you were gonna stop by. I would have made hot chocolate," the young man said with a gentle smile, "I'm Dru, please to meet you," he said holding his hand out.

Penny slowly held her hand out. He shook her hand gently, rubbing his thumb across the top of her hand. He could tell that she was definitely shy.

"Sir! I mean Dru, I'm so sorry and embarrassed," Penny said blushing.

"No worries, lovely."

Penny's heart pounded. As most women, she examined every part of him in less than three seconds. His look was common, a goat-tee, short wavy hair with a slender muscular build, but for Penny he was Prince Charming.

"My God, he's even finer in person," Penny thought as she looked at his black Tee. His jeans were slightly dirty on the knees, but the Egyptian Musk made her look past all of that.

"You live here? She said no worries, didn't I?" Penny could see that was obvious, "I'm sorry, I mean how long have you been here?"

Dru slightly laughed, "None of your business. Now, let's get you down from here. I'll go first. One step at a time," Dru said as he took a few steps down.

Penny slowly turned around, feeling self-conscious about her weight, but that feeling went away as Dru gently held her soft waist. Step by step, her temperature raised.

"He thinks he got all the sense trying to get his feel on with his face next to my ass," Penny thought to herself.

"There that was easy. Now state ya business?" Dru asked standing with his hands behind his back.

Dru was two inches taller than her, so that made Penny feel at ease because she always thought she was too tall. His question caught her off guard.

"Well, I... I," Dru quickly interrupted her bopping his head from side to side repeating her nonsense.

"But I... But I," Dru playfully stammered.

"Shut up," Penny said, and he made her laugh.

"For your info, yeah, I see you smoking ya cigarette every night, so I wanna know what your business is. You gotta problem with that?"

"Oh, now you wanna get jazzy and shit?"

"Well, since I'm jazzy, why didn't you call me?"

"I was gonna get around to it. No worries, remember?"

"What's with him and this no worries stuff," Penny thought to herself.

"Now, you should go now," Dru said.

"Really! He not gonna even ask me out or anything?" Penny thought in disappointment, "oh well, I guess I'll be seeing you around."

"I told you, no worries."

"If he says that shit one more time with that smirk on his face, I'm gonna slap the shit out of his ass!" Penny fumed to herself.

"And by the way, tell your two girlfriends I said hello," Dru said as he opened the door of the basement.

"I'm not gonna tell my friends anything," Penny said but Dru laughed at her again.

"Now you need to stop it with the bullshit!"

"What bullshit?"

"Now you know you gonna run ya pretty ass across the street to your apartment." Penny bit the bottom of her lip trying not to laugh because she knew he was definitely on point.

"Yeah, you'll sit for a minute trying to keep ya mouth shut, but that shit ain't gonna last long. Then ya gonna call ya girls and have a fuckin' squirrel meeting about where I live. But I expect that. Now go and stay sweet."

Penny's heart pounded again because no Black man ever told her to stay sweet. Guys just didn't say those things like that. She really wanted to hug him before she left but she knew that maybe it was too early for that. But he still gave her some more words to make her know she always been noticed by him.

"Oh, by the way, I meant to tell you," Dru started. Penny turned around with a gleaming smile.

"And what might that be Mr. Dru?" Penny asked.

"Quit walking around campus wit cha head down all the time. You're a pretty nice-looking chick."

"Why, thank you," Penny replied.

"Okay well, I'll see you around," Dru said slamming the door. Penny stood by his door confused and bewildered.

"Not only is he mysterious but he's complex and I don't know why."

Penny rushed back to her apartment to do exactly what Dru said she would do. Before Penny could even get her key in the door she was on the phone with Tiffany.

"What's your malfunction? What took so long to call?" Tiffany asked.

"Well excuse me. Everybody doesn't finish exams as fast as you, Ms. Brains. So, what you doin'?" Penny asked.

"Fuckin' around on Facebook," Tiffany said.

Penny couldn't hold it in anymore. "Guess what Girl?" Penny asked excitedly.

"What up?" Tiffany replied.

"I met him today," Penny said.

"Really?! So, who talked to who first? I wanna know everything!"

"Calm down. Actually, I went to go see him," Penny said.

"Where?" Tiffany asked.

"The basement of the P.S. Building."

"Oh yeah, Ebony told me you saw him a couple of nights ago," Tiffany replied. Penny sighed for a moment.

"That big mouth ass bitch, but anyway, I just wanted to see if he worked with maintenance and to introduce myself."

"And what happened?" Tiffany asked.

"Tiff, you can't tell nobody. You promise?" Penny asked.

"Yeah, I promise. So, what happened?" Tiffany eagerly asked.

"You promise? I don't want him to get caught or in trouble," Penny said.

"Damn, I said I promise," Tiffany said.

"Tiff, he lives down there."

"Wait a minute, run that by me one more time. I wanna make sure I heard ya right," Tiffany said.

"Yeah girl, he lives down there."

"Wow! Is he a student?" Tiffany asked.

"I don't know. I didn't get a chance to ask."

"I can't even wrap my mind around that shit. You know if campus police catch him, they're going to lock his ass up?!" Tiffany said while Penny laughed.

"I don't think so. He has a damn miniature studio on the other side of the wall in the basement. The man has a damn MacBook and carpet and shit."

Tiffany laughed out loud, "Are you serious? What's his name?"

"Dru," Penny answered.

"How long has he been there?"

"I don't know. But think about it, we thought he was a student, so ain't no telling. He looks about 23, maybe 24," Penny responded.

"How in the hell does he eat?"

"You act like I gave him a damn cross examination and shit. I don't know. But he's sexy as Heaven, so he must be doing something right."

"Okay, so let's cut to the chase. When is the wedding?" Tiffany jokingly asked.

"You so damn silly. I'm not even going to get my head in the clouds. But enough about that. I gotta call my mom and see if she's going to come here for Thanksgiving. Oh, I almost forgot. Did you get that email from Professor Brooks?" Penny asked.

"Yeah, I did. I don't know where she came up with that shit," Tiffany said while smacking her gum.

"Tiffany, I was reading this assignment and I was like, I can't even catch a sincere date from one of these brothers on campus, let alone do research on one of them. And he can't live on campus anyway."

"Umm, duh silly, why don't you ask Dru?"

CHAPTER 6

Dru and Penny Talks by Text

Penny sat in her living room watching a few snowflakes fall why she thought about how she would ask Dru would he be a part of her project. She should have been ready anyway because she finally got a text message from him.

Dru: Hello Penny, how are you this afternoon?

Penny threw her head back. He would decide to pop up right now, she thought to herself. She automatically knew that it was him by the unknown number.

Penny: I'm fine Dru, and yourself?

Dru: I'm good.

Penny: So, is this your number?

Even though she was glad Dru finally texted she couldn't help to think to herself, *"Where in the hell does, he shower at?"*

Dru: Yes, this is my number for now.

Penny: Oh, okay. So, what are you doing?

Dru: Did you know that something else happened during the Reconstruction era?

"God, I definitely don't feel like talking about the damn Reconstruction era. I just wanna go a damn date, " Penny said to herself.

Penny: Well, I'm familiar but I don't understand the something else you're referring to.

Dru: You're an upcoming anthropologist, you should know these things!

Penny laughed to herself and thought, *"I know he didn't have the nerve to put a damn exclamation point in the message!"*

Penny: How did you know my major is anthropology, Sir!

Dru: First, you need to replace that exclamation point with a question mark. And to answer your question, I saw it on Facebook.

"I see he's a lil smart ass. But I have to say it kinda turns me on," Penny said to herself.

Penny: Well, that's nice to know but the anthropologist doesn't know everything and besides, your question is very vague, Sir!

Dru: Well, the answer is something began to be designed/constructed.

"Well, at least he's got my attention," Penny thought.

Penny: Dru can I ask you a question?

Dru: Sure, I'm all eyes right now.

Penny: I have a research project for my final and I was wondering if I could use you?

Dru: In regard to what? Penny sat nervously hoping that he would say yes.

Penny: Well, I have to spend time with an African American male between the ages of 18 and 30. The project is to observe how the external environment effects your social development in the U.S. By the way, how old are you?

Dru: Sounds interesting. And I'm 25. So, do you understand the designed and constructed era starting at the Reconstruction era?

Penny: No, I don't. Dru, but maybe you can help me out with that. So, do you mind if I use you?

Dru: I'll think about it.

Penny laughed out loud at his response. *"He's such a smart ass!"*

Penny: Well, take your time.

Dru: It's not about the time. Trust me, I have plenty of time. It's about coffee, hot chocolate, or tea. My treat.

Penny was intrigued by the way Dru asked to go on a date and Penny was quick on her feet.

Penny: Of course, I'll have hot chocolate with you.

Dru: Sorry. Straight black coffee for me and hot chocolate for you.

"Ew, yuck! How does he drink straight black coffee," Penny asked herself.

Penny: That's fine. And by the way, I assume this is a date? Because my ass is not climbing that ladder again.

Dru: I kinda figured that. But no worries. Are you familiar with Bucktown?

Penny: I love Bucktown.

Dru: Good! I'll text you the address and we'll meet this Saturday at 1pm sharp! And don't be late.

Penny thought it would be sly to use his own words against him.

Penny: Sure! No worries.

CHAPTER 7

Friday

"There girl, go look in the mirror and tell me how you like it," Tiffany said.

"You think he'll like my hair straight?" Penny asked.

"Of course, just feather the ends before you leave to go meet him."

"You know y'all on some real bullshit," Ebony said as she flipped through an Essence Magazine. Penny and Tiffany laughed because they knew Ebony hated to be the last to find out anything.

"So, we on some bullshit cuz you got a big ass mouth?" Penny asked smiling.

"So, all you're gonna tell me is his name?" Ebony asked while smacking her lips.

"Yes, and that's all you need to know," Penny replied.

"Okay, at least tell me how you got him to ask you out?" Ebony asked.

"Nope. But I will tell you this, he's going to help me with our project for Professor Brooks," Penny said.

"Oh so, you need to paint your nails for that?" Ebony asked.

"You so nosy. And I'm gonna put some lip gloss on too. How about that?" Penny asked.

Even though Tiffany and Ebony were Penny's best friends, Penny knew Ebony couldn't hold water and revealing where he lived might spoil everything. The night fell shortly, Tiffany and Ebony had slept over, but Penny couldn't sleep; so, she sat by the window curled up under her blanket.

Soon Dru came out to smoke his late-night cigarette and Penny's eyes lit up.

"I feel like a spy, but I know he knows, I might be watching," Penny thought to herself.

Penny scrolled through her iPad for a song to play while she sat and watched her dream guy. She felt love in the air, and the best song will be 112's Cupid, as she wondered what he meant by something was designed.

All she could think while the song played was, "Well, maybe his fine ass was designed."

CHAPTER 8

Talented Tenth?

Tiffany parked her car in front of the small coffee shop in town as Penny nervously feathered the ends of her hair.

"So how do I look?" Penny asked while putting some lip gloss on.

"I told you girl; you look fine. You want me to pick you up or you're going to take the train?"

"I'm straight. I'll probably take the train. I'm so nervous," Penny replied, nervously toying with her hair.

"Stop being so nervous. Now, I gotta go, call me when you get back home."

Penny stepped out of the car, looking at herself. Her brown wool sweater matched her hair and tight fitted blue jeans and black pumps seemed good enough for a casual afternoon date. Penny walked in the dim lit coffee shop. It was a jazz coffee shop and Coltrane played in the background, she quickly spotted Dru sitting calmly, smoking a small cigar. Penny walked slowly towards Dru, hoping he liked what she was wearing.

"Well, hello there," Penny said sitting on the leather sofa. She noticed the first thing Dru looked at were her black pumps and gave a slight smile.

"Well, hello there to you too. I like the pumps. Pretty sharp," Dru said.

Penny was impressed to see how Dru dressed outside of the confines of the university. She could tell he had got a fresh haircut. His khakis were creased, and his shoes were tipped shined. His Argyle sweater matched his socks and he sat with one leg crossed over his knee.

"Why thank you. I don't wear pumps that often," Penny said.

"So hot chocolate, correct?"

"That was the plan correct?" Dru signals to the waitress and ordered another coffee and Penny a hot chocolate.

"Well, he dresses much older for his age. My father wears shit like that, " Penny thought as she smiled at Dru's Argyle socks.

"So, what are we working on, love?" Dru asked while rubbing his goatee.

"Oh, so I guess you thought about it?"

"I definitely did. And I'm all about academics. So, the answer is yes. You can use me for your project," Dru replied.

"How old are you again?" Penny asked.

"I'm 25, sweetheart. Why do you ask?" Penny starts to laugh before she could answer.

"I just never see guys your age dress like that. But you look nice."

"Thank you. Now may I see the criteria for this project?"

"Sure," Penny said.

"Well, I can tell he's definitely been to school. He speaks so intelligent. "

"Dru, can I ask you a question?" Penny said.

"Sure, go for it."

"How in the hell did you end up in your situation?" Penny asked.

"Well, you'll probably find all that out later. Isn't that the point of your project? My social development?"

"Damn Penny. That was a stupid ass question, " Penny thought.

"I'm sorry. You're right. I guess we'll get around to that," Penny said.

"Maybe, if I decide to tell you," Dru said with a smirk on his face.

"I see, you're going to make this hard. But I've got plenty of time smart ass," Penny said sipping her hot chocolate.

"How's the hot chocolate?"

"I love it. I could drink hot chocolate even in the summer. But before it slips my mind. What did you mean? Something was designed?" Penny asked.

"Oh, I see that made you think a little. Well, this might get you off to a good start for your project. But most Black men live in a designed mythology which we create on our own."

"Huh?! Dru, you just lost me. What the hell does that mean?" Penny asked while pulling out her pen and notebook.

"No need to write it. It can't be explained."

"Really? Okay, but tell me this, is it a good thing or a bad thing?"

"Well, it's good if it benefits him. But most of the time, it's all about being occupied or should I say gaining recognition from someone else," Dru explained.

"Who?"

"Could be you. Could be the White man, who knows?"

"Well, I might as well let him know," Penny thought.

"Dru, you know I'm mixed?" Penny asked.

"Yes. I kind of figured that out. So, is your mom White or Black?"

"Mom's White and my father is Black," Penny replied.

"Good. Now back to what I was saying. And if we look at the bad part, academics is the only thing that can save him."

"Dru, if you would tell me in detail what the 'created mythology' is, I might."

"No worries sweetheart," Dru said.

"God, I see he's more complex than I thought," Penny said to herself.

"Okay, but I don't think academics is the answer to everything. Don't you think? Uneducated Blacks have no answers, and never will. That's why it's all up to us. Don't you agree?" Dru asked.

"Wow, I can't believe he said that," Penny thought in amazement.

She paused because he still recognized her as a Black woman, an issue she struggled with because she considered herself Black.

"Well, I guess you're right to a degree," Penny said.

"But let's not take up the whole date with this talk."

"Okay, but one more question."

"And what might that be love?" Penny blushed every time he called her love.

"Okay, so you're so passionate about education. Where did you go to college or are you in school now at the campus?" Penny asked.

But to no surprise, Dru became even more complex.

"Well of course, I'm in school, look where I live, and I'm not that passionate, I'm just on my collegiate shit today, you feel me?"

Penny heard what Dru said but at the same time she didn't. Because of something going in one ear and out the other and Dru knew it. He was a sweet talker by nature and could direct the conversation any way he wanted.

"So more hot chocolate honey?" Penny couldn't help but laugh.

"Yes, Dru."

"Now what's so funny?" Dru asked.

"I'm sorry, but guys your age don't say honey, sweetheart, or call a woman "love." It's sweet but it's old fashion," Penny answered.

"Trust me love, I'm not that old fashioned, you will see. By the way, when shall we meet again?"

"I don't know, probably after Thanksgiving and what are you doing for the holidays?" Penny asked nervously. She didn't know if he had family or not, but as usual, Dru just sat with a smirk on his face.

"No worries, just black coffee, cigarettes, and probably a Snickers bar," he replied.

"You serious?"

"Sure, holidays left my mind, a long time ago."

Penny could see that it would have been useless to invite him to her house for the holidays, but Dru taking her out for hot chocolate was a holiday by itself. Some things were meant to be left alone, but in the days to come, Penny is going to soon find out that Dru's mind tops all holidays. An hour had passed and the best part of any first date would be how it would end.

"So, you feel like riding the train back with me?" Penny asked.

Since Dru lived across the street from her she automatically assumed he would take her home. But she was really sadly mistaken.

"No sweetheart, you go now and make it home safe. I'll be having one more cup."

"Is he serious? He already drank three damn cups!" Penny thought, trying to hold her disappointment in.

"You're sure?"

"Definitely sure. But you make it home safe and make sure you call me with our schedule."

"I could just slap his ass. He's supposed to at least walk me to the train," Penny silently fumed.

But Dru was still a gentleman and walked her to the door of the coffee shop and gave her a tight hug.

"Now, you be safe now til next time."

"Well, I guess I can't complain. At least he did that," Penny said to herself.

Dru stood in the window of the coffee shop, watching Penny, until he saw her get on the train.

"Well, I can tell she's the one, a mixture of the two, and I'm of many, maybe thousands I didn't expect this, but I have no choice," Dru thought as he looked at the grey cloudy sky with a smile.

CHAPTER 9

Ma'at's Law

"Guide her and take her to any experience you choose, but you are not to lay a hand of intimacy on her. For her heart is pure."

CHAPTER 10

Five Days Before Thanksgiving

Penny rushed in her apartment and quickly turned her space heater on. It was five days before Thanksgiving, and she had to pack but she couldn't wait to call Tiffany to tell her about her date. Not one full ring went by before Tiffany answered.

"So, tell me what happened? What's he like and don't leave out nothing!" Tiffany said excitedly.

"Damn Girl, you starting to get worse than Ebony but anyway, I had a lovely time and yes he's a sweetheart," Penny said as she curled up on her sofa.

As she looked out the window, she saw Dru flicking his cigarette on the ground and she shot down the stairs.

"What the hell?" Penny asked out loud.

"Hello, you there?" Tiffany asked. Penny paused trying to figure out how Dru beat her home.

"Yeah, I'm here. I just saw Dru."

"Oh, he drove you home?" Tiffany asked.

"No, Tiff, I left him at the coffee shop."

"Well, maybe he drives."

"I don't know but..."

"Enough about that. I know what you're gonna say he could've at least drove you home. So, what happened?" Tiffany asked.

Penny still stared at the spot where Dru was smoking, puzzled, because she had a feeling, he didn't have a car and even if he took another route on the bus, he still wouldn't have beat her home.

"Yeah, I was gonna say that but he's nice and we just talked."

"That's it?!" Tiffany exclaimed.

"Yeah, he's gonna let use him for my final."

"And," Tiffany said anxiously.

"And what? Damn, you act like we were supposed to have hot sex in the bathroom," Penny said.

"Well, that would have been nice too."

"Shut up you're so silly," Penny said.

"Did he tell you why he's living under the damn college?" Tiffany asked.

"No Tiff, I didn't get that far, but he's definitely not what expected."

"What you mean?"

"Girl, he's smart and shit I really don't know what happened to him but I guess I'll find all that out later. But I'm gotta go pack. I'll call you tomorrow when I get to my mom's," Penny said.

"Okay, love ya Sis." Penny had really made up an excuse so she could text Dru.

Penny: Excuse me Sir but how did you get home so fast?

Dru: Excuse me Miss but you could have called. You women today got it real bad with the texting thing. But to answer your question no worries.

"God, he makes me sick!" Penny thought.

Penny: Well, I was just letting you know that I got in and I'm leaving for my mom's tomorrow. You sure you won't be lonely for the holidays?

Dru: Ain't no pressure love. By the way I meant to tell you that I'm very intrigued with your assignment.

Penny: Really? I'm so glad you are.

Dru: Definitely am. We both have to make a grade. An A+ for you, of course.

Penny: Of course, I've never had a B in anything. What's the grade you have to make?

Dru: Did you know many African American men are nothing more than a big pot of gumbo? Penny couldn't help but to laugh out loud.

Penny: Gumbo? That's a weird analogy.

Dru: Only thing I could think of. Lots of ingredients.

Penny: And what are the ingredients if you don't mind me asking?

Dru: No worries. You'll see, now you have a lovely holiday.

Penny: Okay I'll call you later.

"Boy he's one of a kind," Penny said to herself.

CHAPTER 11

Two Days Before Thanksgiving

It was two days before Thanksgiving for Penny. It was a time to relax and break free from all academics. Penny's parents, Renee and Anthony were both architects and an interracial couple that lived on the North Side of Oak Park where Penny grew up. Penny's parents always felt pressure about interracial relationships and thought it was best to raise a mixed child in a mixed upper middle-class suburb, such as Oak Park. Most of the houses ranged no less than $350,000 or better.

Anthony and Renee were both in their mid-50s and met in college. They had both graduated from the Illinois Institute of Technology on Chicago Southside and both agreed in college that they only wanted one child, and their blessing was Penny.

Penny grew up as a common daddy's girl. Penny like most daughters had a strong bond with her father, most of all, because early in her childhood, he always taught her that she was a Black girl and so never get confused like most of her mixed friends were. Renee never struggled with Anthony because who would know best, other than a White woman that her racially mixed child might be viewed as White in Europe, but in America, Penny would be viewed as Black. For the most part, Penny's parents planned and understood that identity was the most important.

Penny stayed in her room listening to all her younger cousins running through the house while thinking about Dru.

"Now why hasn't his ass called me?" Penny thought scrolling through her iPhone. Penny heard a gentle knock on the door before her mother crept in her bedroom.

"Hey, Mom," Penny greeted her.

"I see you're hiding out. You want to come help with the dressing?" Penny's mother asked.

Penny took a deep breath. "Mom, don't you hate the cat and mouse game?" Renee seemed to laugh because she could tell Penny was having boy problems.

"It's time for a mother daughter talk, huh? Sounds like my little girl has a boyfriend. So, who is he?"

"Well, he's not my boyfriend," Penny replied.

"What's his name?" Renee asked while curling up next to Penny. She loved to have talks like this one.

"His name is Dru."

"Oh, is it short for Andru?"

"Actually, I don't know. And I don't know his last name," Penny replied.

"Well, he must be special because he's definitely on your mind."

"Yeah, I'm using him for my project. My professor has us examining a Black male dealing with social development in America."

"Wow, that sounds interesting. Now come on tell mom about the cat and mouse game."

"Mommy, he took me on a date on Saturday, but he doesn't really text me or call me much, and he knows I like him. Sometimes I wonder, does he think I don't like him because of his situation."

"And what's his situation?"

Penny always put her thumbnail in her mouth when she really didn't want to talk about something.

"He's homeless mom."

"Oh Wow, so where does he sleep?"

Penny still had to sort of laugh and Renee gave a puzzled smile because homelessness definitely wasn't a laughing matter.

"I'm sorry mom for laughing but he lives in the basement of the Political Science Building, and no I don't know how long he's been there."

"Well, I don't know how well your father would have taken this, but you could've invited him."

"Nope, he doesn't celebrate Thanksgiving, I thought of that already," Penny replied.

Renee rubbed Penny's hair softly. "Well, that is complex but I will tell you this cat and mouse game can be good if he is the mouse."

"Okay, mom I gotta hear this one."

"Sometimes we can be the cat chasing the mouse."

"And?"

"Well, the mouse is hard to catch because the mouse isn't always available."

"Mom, I don't get it."

"It means a man that's not always available and is always busy is a good man. You'll understand one day. We hate men who never have any business. So be patient, he'll call."

"But mom..."

"Trust me, Honey, real man don't chase women. He's just busy, he'll call, trust me. Now I gotta get back in the kitchen and you know your father will be up here soon as I say you don't want to help in the kitchen."

"God, I know."

"But I'm not gonna say anything about Dru. Now give me some sugar."

Penny couldn't help but take her mother's advice. The only thing to ease Penny's mind would be the box of chocolate covered cherries her father left for her. She could always expect a box of some sort of candy every time she came home for the holidays. Penny already had made up her mind, she wasn't helping in the kitchen, and the only thing left to do, was to enjoy her cherries and put on her favorite movie Trading Places. She was always fond of actors and she always had an abstract way of thinking. I wondered do actors get so caught up in roles that they forget who they are. It was a question she always asked herself when she watched what was considered flawless acting, but it didn't take long for her to be interrupted by Jocelyn, her five-year-old cousin on her father's side. Jocelyn only stood about three feet, and she had just lost her two front teeth, which tickled Penny. Jocelyn hopped in her bed.

"Gimme one," Joselyn said demanding a cherry.

"Um, excuse me number one, you didn't knock and number two say please." Joselyn quickly folded her hands smiling.

"I see you lost something," Penny said.

"Yup! My teeth see!" Penny couldn't help but to laugh.

"So, where's your bad brother at?"

"I don't know."

"Good, don't talk his butt up!"

Penny rolled her eyes. Emilly was her other cousin. An eight-year-old who was a Holy terror. Penny's mom always said he was so bad he'd probably get kicked out of Hell. Penny knew Joselyn wasn't going to leave anytime soon and even though she couldn't pay attention to her favorite movie, just having it on relaxed her and as her mother reminded her, her father would soon join her anyway.

"Well, here comes dad, I can smell that damn pipe tobacco," Penny thought to herself as she sat up and waited for his knock.

Since she wasn't a smoker, she could smell him a mile away. One thing she was used to is that he never knocked. He would always creep in slowly.

"Well, there's my favorite daughter," Anthony said.

"Hey Dad, by the way, I'm your only daughter."

Anthony was a tall man with a dark complexion and broad shoulders. He had the typical build of a football player. His hair was short and fully gray, including his beard. Penny was always amused because he never changed his style, even when he say on the end of her bed, he always put his glasses on the tip of his nose and crossed his leg over his knee, and he always started his father daughter talk the same way from the day she started high school.

"So, I don't have to go get my gun, do I?"

Penny burst up laughing. "No Dad, you don't have to go get your gun. You always say that."

"I know but it's lots of guys in college and..."

"Yes, I know if they wanna take me out they have to go through your examination." Penny always sat back and smiled because she knew that he was old fashion and would never change.

"Absolutely."

Penny couldn't help but to bite her lips to keep from laughing because he always gave her the same lecture.

"Absolutely! He has to go through my examination, then I'll deem him qualified."

"Deem Dad???"

"Oh God, I don't know why I said that he's gonna be in here for about two more hours!"'

"Yes! You know the deal! He must be willing to marry correct?"'

"Yes, Dad."

"Because ain't no man gonna be shakin' and bakin' making babies with my daughter and he's not willing to marry, correct?"'

"Yes Dad, are you done?" Anthony gave her a smile; he knew she hated when he gave her his talk.

"So, how's school?"'

"Fine, as usual, gotta new project nothing too hard though."

"Yes, your mother was telling me."

Penny knew for starters her dad would have never approved of Dru just off the fact that he was homeless and nobody would've have even been good enough for his only daughter. Penny begun to get nervous as her dad sat for a moment just smiling as if he knew something.

"So, you wanna tell me more about this project of yours?"

"God, I bet mom told him!"

"No, it's nothing that complicated Dad; nothing I won't get an 'A' in."

Penny hoped that would throw him off from asking anymore questions and she succeeded.

"Well, that's my girl. Now you sure you don't wanna help in the kitchen?"'

"No Dad, I'm okay but I promise to help with the dressing promise."

Penny quickly gave her dad a hug while her phone rang. She saw it was no one other than Dru. The ringtone in her earpiece rang three times and it seemed like it was taking her dad forever to leave the room probably because he had Jocelyn who had fallen asleep over his shoulder. As soon as her door closed, she cleared her throat and gave Dru a whispering hello; so afraid that her dad would hear. She knew a hello to Tiffany or Ebony was totally different than a hello to a guy she has a crush on.

"Well, hello to you too Miss Penny, just calling to check on you."

"Yes! Well, he must be starting to get interested if he's checking on me," Penny thought.

"I'm fine Dru. So, what cha doing?"

"So far, the night is good, besides my heater breaking."

"Wow Dru, it's definitely too cold out; you gonna be alright tonight?"

"No worries. I'll be fine. Besides, your voice will keep me warm for a few minutes."

"That was so sweet," Penny thought as she puckered her glass lips, wishing she could kiss him for saying such a thing.

"I have more than a few minutes for you."

"That's good. So, we'll be starting when you get back, I assume?"

"Yes, and I have a lot of questions."

"Oh, about my life, but I think it's best if we skip all that for a while and we should just hang out."

Penny had become confused. She felt frustration because just hanging out without knowing Dru's case history would make her assignment even harder.

"Umm Dru, I'm going to have to know some history to start. Don't you think?"

"No worries, just take a walk with me and everything will fall in your lap."

"Okay, Dru, you're the boss. What do you mean take a walk with you?"

"Can I ask you a question?"

"Sure Dru, of course."

"When do you think the Black man's, neurotic drama begins?"

"Uh, I don't know what the hell that means."

"Dru what's a neurotic drama?"

Penny could hear Dru flicking his lighter and a slight laugh as if she should know what he was talking about.

"Did you know that any Black child that comes in contact with the White world without being taught about it first will turn his entire lifespan into a drama?" Penny quickly grabbed her notebook to jot down what Dru said before she would forget.

"Okay, where did all this come from and what do you mean a White world?"

"There! It just needed some electrical tape."

"Dru I know you didn't just ignore me."

"No, not at all. But you have a lot to learn, so I'll leave you with this, the White world is played at through the Black man's behavior, get it?"

"No Dru, wait I don't get it."

"Well, you get some rest."

"Dru you better not go, now explain."

"You can't explain it with words, just take a walk with me. Now, I'll text you later and have a lovely Thanksgiving." Before Penny could say goodbye, the phone went dead.

"God, I hate when he does that shit!"

In her moment of frustration, Tiffany was always an open ear to talk to. Penny re-read the words neurotic drama over and over while Tiffany's phone rang. Penny could tell by the noise in the background Tiff was around her entire family.

"What's up girl?"

"Nothing girl, can you go in another room? I need to talk." Tiffany could hear in Penny's voice that whatever it was, it couldn't wait.

"Okay, I'm in the guest room now. So, what's going on, girl?"

"I just got off the phone with Mr. You-Know-Who." Tiffany couldn't help but to laugh.

"So, what did Mr. Philosophical have to say now?"

"Okay, you ready for this?"

"Yes, shoot."

"So, we were talking about my assignment and he turns around and says the Black man is going through a neurotic drama."

"Damn, girl. I don't know what the hell that means. Okay, but..."

"But hold on Tiff, he said it begins when a Black child enters the White world stop laughing!"

"I'm sorry, but you got your hands full."

"Can I tell you something to Tiff?"

"Yeah, I know you're falling for him."

"You know I am but it's something like magical or I mean, mysterious about him. Maybe my women's intuition is kicking in or something."

"Maybe."

"Girl, I feel like telling him to pack up all that bullshit..."

"Penny now stop that. Don't let his ass move in, you too damn nice." Penny sighed trying not to follow her heart.

"Plus, you don't know how long he's been homeless. He'll probably eat up all your food and shit."

"Tiff, you so damn silly."

"Yeah, I know. I'm just saying, take it slow. Obviously, he's been doing okay before y'all met. You feel me?"

"Yeah, I guess you're right. But when break is over, you know, we'll still have bout three to four days left. I might invite him over for lunch or something. What cha think?"

"I guess that's cool and besides, I know you girl you gonna do it anyway. Now I gotta go, call me tomorrow."

"K love ya."

Talking to Tiffany was always soothing even though she didn't have an answer to what a neurotic drama is; so, she knew she was bound to Dru's rule to just take a walk with him.

CHAPTER 12

Our Dinner Date

Thanksgiving came and went, Penny left home early to make sure the next three days could be spent with the Dru. She had made it home to her cozy apartment. It was Friday evening and Penny has spent all day preparing what was supposed to be lunch turned into dinner. She was so pleased that Dru didn't hesitate to have dinner at her apartment and Dru was definitely on time for his eight o'clock dinner appointment.

Penny sat in her bedroom looking at her shape in the mirror, and her college sweat suit that hugged every curve of her body was okay for her. She was a BBW with no stomach. Tiffany and Ebony always were envious, especially Ebony, as to how Penny could eat anything and have a flat stomach. Penny took one last glance, hugged her ass with hands, and she couldn't have help but to have put a push-up bra on. Every woman knows no man cannot stop looking at 36DD breasts in a push-up bra. She knew her heart had fallen for him. She knew because even his knock at the door made her heart pound. (KNOCK-KNOCK)

Penny took a deep breath as she slipped her plush Bugs Bunny house shoes on. Penny opened her door with a gleaming smile that was dropped dead gorgeous.

"Hey Dru."

"Well, hello there, Miss Penny," Dru said with a cup of coffee in his hands.

"Come on in and make yourself at home. I hope you like steak," Penny said and even she had noticed her voice sounded nervous.

Dru walked slowly towards her couch. Penny noticed that he was dressed simpler than how he was dressed at the coffee shop. He wore some loose fitted jeans, the latest Air Max's and a hooded Timberland sweatshirt.

"Well, I see he has a well picked out wardrobe and he got his haircut. God! I love waves, " Penny thought, "so do you like steak?"

"Sure," Dru said as he leaned back on the couch, crossing his leg.

"Why you got that smirk on your face?" Penny asked.

"Because I can see you went through a whole lot of trouble."

"It's nothing and I hope you like mashed potatoes and salad, "Penny said placing his plate in front of him. She thought it would be ladylike to sit on the far end of the couch.

"You know you can scoot your ass a little closer. I'm not gonna bite."

Penny suddenly felt embarrassed because she didn't expect him to say that. But she still wanted to play hard to get.

"Umm excuse me, Scoot my ass?"

"Yeah, scoot cha' ass a little closer and stop being such a sour puss."

Penny bit the bottom of her lip trying not to laugh, but she knew deep down she liked his bossiness. So, she did as she was told and slid closer to him, still staying at least a foot away.

"Is that better?"

"This steak is bomb sweetheart," Dru said.

"I see he has selective hearing or maybe my steak is that good!"

"So, are we supposed to be starting?" Dru asked.

"Dru it's eight o'clock in the evening. I was going to say we could start tomorrow, or I should say take our little walk, right?"

"Absolutely. By the way I like that door," Dru said as he stuffed steak and salad in his mouth.

"So, you mean to tell me out of all this stuff in my apartment, you like my door? Really, Dru?"

"No, I'm serious."

"Okay, why?"

Penny knew by now his response was not going to be an ordinary one. Dru quickly directed Penny's attention pointing at the door.

"The door that leads to the outside world is always the transition state."

"God here we go with this shit!" Penny sighed.

"Okay, what's the transition state, Dru?"

"You'll see now eat ya steak, it's getting cold."

Penny could already sense that whatever Dru had in store for her was going to take her to another level, but she didn't know why. The only thing would be to go with the flow. A couple of hours had passed. Penny learned they both like the same movies. And that was about as far as it went. Ten o'clock had rolled around, and Dru or Penny hadn't noticed the snowstorm that hit.

"Damn Dru, look! It's snowing like hell," Penny stood for a moment staring at the snowflakes mixed with icy rain and a sudden urge came over her. Regardless of what Tiffany said, Penny did the exact opposite.

"Dru, can I ask you a question?" Penny asked as she sat back next to Dru, only this time, she sat just a little closer.

"Sure," Dru said finishing the last bit of steak.

"Would you like to stay for the weekend? I mean, just to get out that cold basement." Dru gave Penny a very puzzling look as if she was crazy.

"Now what possessed you to make such an offer? You really don't know me you're that comfortable with me so soon?"

"Obviously, I think you're harmless if I invited you to my house."

"Most people don't do shit like this."

"Well, I'm not like most and..."

"Then enough said. I'll be right back; I need a change of clothes."

Penny stood in sort of a gaze watching Dru zip his hoodie. She didn't really expect him to accept her invite so quickly.

"Wait, Dru, I got something for you I got a skullcap for you."

Penny quickly ran to her room to rumble through some of her clothes, but it didn't matter because she had her front door open.

"Damn, I guess he said to hell with the hat," Penny thought, but something caught her attention that made her body freeze.

"What the hell is all that noise," Penny wondered.

When her door opened, it seemed as if she was on the bottom floor of her building. She heard sirens and people fighting and cussing in the background. When her door shut, the noise disappeared. Penny quickly came out of her room. It was impossible to hear that noise so close because she lived on the eighth floor. Penny walked slowly to her door and opened it slowly, peeking out into the empty hallway.

"That's impossible," Penny thought as she went to her patio window to find the street was clear.

No sirens, no people, just Dru walking across the streets to get his clothes. Penny sat on her love seat thinking to herself. Maybe I'm just tripping and she left it at that. Dru was back in almost five minutes. This time he didn't knock. Penny was startled for a moment to see Dru had bought a giant army duffel bag. She had remembered he had about three but this bag was rather huge.

"Damn Dru, I said just the weekend. That's a lot, don't you think?" Penny asked as she heard Tiffany's voice in her head, "you know he'll eat up all your food and shit."

"So where do I sleep?" Dru asked as he threw his bag in the corner; he even brought his laptop.

"You can sleep on a couch."

"Damn, this is what I get for being a damn good citizen. I don't think I was for real when I asked him."

"And it's a pullout."

"That's what's up."

Penny kind of calmed down. Besides what homeless person wouldn't want to be in a warm place during a snowstorm. He began to act as if they had known each other forever.

"Got any beer?" Penny laughed because she wasn't ready for that either.

"Sure, I got some Heineken in the fridge here, you sit..."

"No, I'll show myself to the fridge. Heineken for you too, correct?"

"Okay, yes, I guess."

Penny just smiled as she watched Dru rumble through her refrigerator. Well, I can say he's definitely down to earth and I bet not drink more than two, I already want to pounce on his fine ass! Dru hurried back, tilting the neck bottle as far as he could go.

"There, I opened yours for you."

"Thanks."

"What's so funny?"

"Oh, nothing, it's just oh, never mind."

"So, what time do we start?"

"Whatever time you like."

"Then let's head out about one o'clock."

"Okay, but where are we going?"

"I don't know, I haven't decided."

Penny sat watching Dru pulled the couch out into a bed. She could tell he was anxious and she desperately wanted to ask him when the last time he slept in a real bed.

"Dru?"

"What, love?"

"How long have you been homeless?"

"You get some blankets?"

"There you go with your selective hearing."

"No, I heard you. But the correct question is when did I check out of society?"

"Here's some blankets. I never heard it put that way."

"Oh, so when..."

"That's not important. We should just stick to your assignment."

"Well, that didn't work," Penny thought.

"Okay, how do you get money?"

"That's the least of my worries."

"So, you don't worry about money?"

"What homeless person does?"

"Fuck, he's complex!"

"You sure are a nosy little thing," Dru said as he laid back placing his hands behind his head with a slight devious smile. He could tell Penny's attention had shifted to his biceps.

"You okay, sweetheart?"

"Oh, I'm sorry. What was I saying?"

"You were talking about my money situation which I have no worries.

So, what's your next question?"

"Shut up don't say it like that like I'm bothering you and stop laughing!" She could see that he did enjoy her questions, even though she never got a full answer or at least one to her satisfaction.

"Okay, one last question and I'll leave you alone."

"Okay."

"Most homeless people sleep on the train or a shelter. Why the college?"

"Umm, light bulb, sweetheart even though I checked out doesn't mean I'm not supposed to keep up with the world and what better place but the college." Penny sipped her beer, every response he gave began to intrigue her more and more.

"I don't get and don't be saying light bulb like I'm slow or something," Penny said rolling her neck flirtatiously.

"Well, the train goes in a big damn circle all day and shelters are too depressing. I'm always in tune with the world as long as I'm around a college, makes sense?"

"Then why don't you just go to school, Dru?"

"You said only one more question. Now unlike you, it's time for me to rest. I'll see you in the morning."

Within a second Penny watched as he put his Du-Rag on as if she was no longer there. No goodnight, he just got under the blanket and turned over. The absurd thing is, she had never seen anyone fall asleep as soon as they closed their eyes. It was like he was a narcoleptic.

"I don't believe his ass just turned over and went to sleep. Huh... talk about take advantage of a home cooked meal and a warm bed... at least he didn't bullshit around."

Penny stood over Dru for a moment to rub his forehead. Since she was a night owl, she knew she had to call Tiffany. Penny tip-toed back to her room, waiting patiently for Tiffany to pick up. More than likely, she was awake because it was always an everlasting party whenever Tiffany went home for the holidays, but Penny became a little startled that Tiffany was actually asleep.

"Hello, what girl?" Tiffany said.

"Damn, what the hell you doin' sleep?"

"Man, I got drunk wit my cousins and you know how that go. So, what's good?" Penny paused a moment, biting her pinky nail, prepared for drama.

"Okay... you're gonna be mad."

"You fucked him already?!"

Penny threw her head back in amazement because even though of course she thought about it, that was the last thing on her mind (at least for the time being).

"Tiff... I thought you knew me better than that."

"Okay, I'm sorry, but I don't know what else I could be mad about."

"He's here," Penny interrupted quickly as if Tiff didn't hear her.

"Run that by me again?"

"In my living room sleep."

"Girl... no you didn't! You let him move in?"

"Naw girl... I just let him stay for the weekend. Trust me, he's cool."

"Okay, so after everything I..."

"Yeah Tiff, I know, but it started snowing and..."

"Yeah whatever girl. You too damn nice and you still probably don't know his full name, do you?"

"No, but...'

"Exactly my point. I know y'all went out on a date but really you got a total stranger in ya living room."

"Tiff he's such a sweetheart though... God, you know how bad I wanna spoil a man?"

"Girl, I ain't mad but I'm definitely coming over. Me and Ebony on Sunday, cool?"

"You just trying to be nosy... I'll think about it, but I'm a let cha' go, we got a big day tomorrow."

"Oh, well excuse me," Tiff said sarcastically.

"Okay, just call me anyway, love ya."

The line went dead and Penny laid staring at the ceiling in wonder. For some reason, the last thought that went through her mind was, *"Penny, what have you gotten yourself into?"*

CHAPTER 13

The Next Morning

It was 11:00 a.m. and Penny rolled over slowly looking out her window. She gave a slight smile. It was a beautiful cold morning and the entire sky was blue. Still anticipating where she and Dru would venture out to, she already planned out what she would wear. Penny was always a simple girl and opted for a grey wood turtleneck sweater that looked good for a cold day, paired with blue jeans and her leather high heeled grey boots. She figured her ensemble would look good with whatever Dru was wearing.

Since she had her bathroom attached to her room, she thought it would be best to take a quick shower, get dressed, and make Dru some breakfast.

A half hour shower and a half hour to get dressed was good timing and she still had to make some breakfast.

Penny sat in her loveseat, watching the clock, as she rubbed shea butter on her feet. It was noon and time to get Dru up. Before she left her room, she grabbed the half empty Heineken that she never finished. She opened the door slowly to see if Dru was still asleep, but her eyes widened to see that the couch was made.

"Now I know he didn't leave," Penny thought to herself.

"Dru!" Penny called out walking slowly wondering where Dru was, but he was there as she turned and looked in the guest bathroom.

Dru was grooming himself and Penny's mouth widened as she dropped the Heineken bottle in shock on the carpeted floor. She looked at Dru from head to toe in full shock and he gave a slight smile as he looked at her reflection in the mirror.

"How do I look, shawty?" Dru asked as he swerved his hips from side to side.

Penny covered her mouth for a moment. She was frozen. This wasn't the same guy that took her out for hot chocolate and he sure as hell wasn't the same guy, she left in the living room the night before.

"Umm, I guess you look fine," Penny said as she examined Dru's pearly white Air Force One's, Polo jeans sagged to mid-thigh, red Coogi sweater and his Du-Rag that was un-tied where the strings draped either side of his shoulders.

"Yeah, shawty fine at the word, ya dig?"

Penny stood with her mouth wide open, slowly picking the bottle off the floor. She didn't know what to say. His vocabulary had changed and all she could do was go along with it.

"Maybe this is how he is for real I guess," she thought.

"Dru you hungry?" Penny asked. She still couldn't keep from smiling at Dru's appearance.

"So, he's really a thug on the inside," she surmised.

"Naw Baby, it's that time. We'll cop a bite to eat while we're out." Penny quickly grabbed her Coach purse.

"Okay, I'm ready." But Dru stood silently staring at the door in a hypnotic state. Penny waved her hand in front of his face.

"Hello, you ready?"

"Sure love," Dru said with his usual sly smile. He gently took Penny by the hand which made her snatch away because his hands were ice cold.

"Damn why are your hands so cold?"

Dru quickly ignored her and took her by the hand. His pace was swift. Penny felt like a little girl being dragged behind and when he opened the door, her life would change forever.

CHAPTER 14

Chicago's West Side

As they stepped from her apartment, Dru dragged her so fast she didn't even have time to think. All she knew she was not in her hallway. The frigid wind slapped her in the face. She went from her apartment door to the heart of Chicago's west side. Dru quickly shut the door. Penny's heart raced. She felt like she was Alice in Wonderland. There was traffic everywhere and when she looked up at the street sign, she was on Lake and Pulaski. She saw the drug dealers on the corner; people scrambling to cop the best dope; people running out the fast food restaurant. Dru stood looking at her chewing a piece of bubble gum, smiling while he looked at his chrome watch.

"Dru! How the fuck did you do that?!

Penny took two steps back as if Dru were the devil. When she turned to look back at the door, they were standing in front of an abandoned building and three old men with crack pipes in their hands. Of course, they stopped and looked as if she had interrupted the party.

"Oh! I'm so sorry," Penny said as she stepped back, looking at Dru. She quickly took a deep breath.

"Who are you?"

"Bout time you came to ya mutha fuckin' senses," Dru said with a bossy attitude, only this time it didn't turn Penny on.

"How did you do that? Who are you?"

Dru ignored her and started to walk as if he knew she had no choice but to follow.

"Man bring ya pretty ass on! I gotta go see what's up wit my niggaz you can stand there lookin' stupid if you want shorty!"

Penny watched as Dru walked away and definitely wasn't waiting and she knew however he had the power to switch dimensions at will, she was stuck. Penny quickly ran behind him trying to keep her balance of course, her high heeled boots definitely weren't made for Dru's pace.

"Dru wait, why you walking so fast? Were you taking me?"

But Dru still ignored her. He still took her by the hand. The next thing she knew Dru was standing in front of two older gentlemen, both in their late fifties, and Penny could see they apparently knew Dru.

"What up, fiz-ool?!" one of the older gentlemen said to Dru. Penny had seen men like this before but only in the 1970's pimp movies, but she paid more attention to Dru because his style changed even more.

"What Chin-nolly, y'all coolin'?

"Too cool fa school, ya dig?"

Penny couldn't help but to keep a ladylike smile as she examined the two men.

"Oooh wee who is this pretty lil flower?" One of the men said looking at Penny.

"Yeah dis my prizzize possession ya dig?" Dru said and Penny looked at him with flared nostrils of anger.

"Now I know these old ass men are fucking pimps, fuck does he mean his prized possession?"

"Oooh Wee! See I like the youngster, he's going places, by the way, call me P-Goldie. Hey youngsta, gimme some skin. You caught cha dizime," P-Goldie said as he giggled.

Penny was quite amused because he had a devious smile, his fingernails were longer than hers, he wore his hat like an elf hat, and every time he laughed, he bent his knees and moved his hips from side to side, and his green gators standing pigeon-toed he took small little baby steps back and forth.

"Hi, I'm Penny, nice to meet you," Penny said taking a deep breath, trying not to laugh in his face.

She noticed the other gentlemen didn't talk, he just scrolled though his phone.

"A'ight, Popz, me and da lady gotta jet, ya feel me? Always come check on old skool catz," Dru said as he stood holding his crotch, another thing that made Penny's eyes buck, but it didn't stop there.

The other gentlemen who was seemingly quiet around his cell phone since he had an earpiece, Penny became amazed as he talked and he combed his permed hair to the back. It was perfectly laid and with every stroke, he made sure the duck tail stayed curled in the back.

Penny couldn't help but watch his every move. He had the same stance as P-Goldie, pigeon-toed with brown gators, only difference was he tucked both his middle fingers in the palm and stomped his heel on the ground as he spoke. Apparently, one of his hoes didn't make the grade.

"Bitch! What da fuck you mean?" Penny eyes got bug as saucers because the closest thing to what she was listening to would have been old pimp movies.

"Excuse me, Dru. Excuse me Baby girl," the older pimp said staring at Penny.

"Well at least he apologized for his language," Penny thought.

"Naw bitch! I'm C-Money bitch! You know the mutha fuckin' deal!" C-Money paused and Penny wished she could what his ho was saying but it didn't get any better.

"Bitch, fuck you mean on $500? Naw bitch! You not speakin' my language, ya dig? Bitch that pussy a rack, bitch! You was late, that's ya mutha fuckin' problem," C-Money said.

Penny noticed he stomped his every time he said bitch and he purposely became knock-kneed.

"Bitch I bitch, check dis out, ain't sunny days when I see ya I wouldn't give a damn if it was snowin' bitch! You betta walk in between da mutha fuckin' snowflakes!! Now bring me my money!"

Dru slightly leaned over to Penny's ear, "Come on baby girl, lets cop a bite to eat."

Once again, Penny felt herself being dragged across the street and she followed. Dru walked fast as usual, unzipping his hoodie, his Jesus medallion that hung almost to his belt, swung back and forth like a Big Ben clock, and now she found herself in the Korean restaurant. It was crowded and as soon as they walk through the door, she saw Dru take a stack of money out his pocket within two seconds. Twenty dollars went in one hand and a sack of weed back to Dru's hand.

"Oh wow, I know his ass didn't just do this in front of me," Penny thought.

"Dru I wanna..."

"Yeah, so what cha want? No worries, I got this," Dru said as he went to the counter where a small Korean guy stood with a gentle smile.

"Take your order?"

"Yeah, give me two three-piece with mild sauce on the fries and two grape pops, and hurry the fuck up!"

"Dru, why did you say that?" Penny whispered.

"Be cool Shorty, I got this."

The Korean hurried back and slid the food across the counter. Not only did Penny's mind adapt quickly to what she thought was a dream world, but the next time she looked at Dru had taken her to the top of the building nearby. She could tell Dru probably smoked his weed occasionally for privacy when they got to the top of the five-story building through the fire escape Dru sat on the edge of the building, letting his feet dangle from the rooftop.

"Come on babe, sit. Shoulda have told you not to wear no fucking high heeled boots for a walk."

"Dru I'm not sitting on the edge of this building, I'm afraid of heights."

"Girl sit cha ass down, I gotcha trust me," Dru said licking his freshly rolled blunt.

"We not gonna get in trouble up here?" Penny asked as Dru held her waist.

"Dru if I fall, I'll kill you."

"Sorry babe, if you fall, you'll be dead anyway but anyway, you drink?"

When Penny looked in between them, Dru had placed a pint of Hennessy on the ledge.

"Where the hell you get that from?"

"I been had it, go head so we can talk social development."

Penny stared at the bottle for a moment while Dru blew smoke in the air. It was like the 20-degree weather didn't even faze him. Penny was just a social drinker but she knew a shot of Henn would probably warm her up.

"Okay fine, you got a cup? Dru gave a slight chuckle.

"Quit fuckin' playing and tilt the damn bottle damn you green fa real."

"Don't call my ass green." Penny took a small sip and Dru rolled his eyes at her, and Penny sat and stared at Dru, and the same question came to her.

"Dru are you an angel or something? Cuz I know I ain't trippin'."

"You adapt quick. Most people would still be runnin' down the block. You took it well," Dru said as he lit his Newport.

Penny laughed. The little shot of Hennessy calmed her down.

"So, this is real?"

"Of course, your assignment is to see how my mind is socially developed, right?" Penny put her head down, shaking it from left to right, still confused.

"Okay, so let me get this straight is this your mind?"

"Yup, and you win the $100,000 prize," Dru said sarcastically.

"Dru, shut up, quit making fun of me. So, this is your mind?"

Dru made things more complex for Penny. She couldn't discern if he was high or sober but either way she froze in amazement when Dru burst into laughter and began to rap the hook from Nas' Illmatic, Whose World is This?

"Whose World is This? The World is Yours! The World is Yours! It's Mine, Mine, It's Mine. Whose World is This!" Penny placed her index finger under her nose.

"Dru, I've heard that song, and I didn't think you or I were even old enough to remember it."

"Who cares about how old it is. It's part of the social development, get it?" But Dru didn't stop there. For some reason she could tell he had music playing in his head.

"Thug Life! On Dat Thug Life!" Penny took another sip and interrupted Dru in his glory.

"Dru the world isn't operating off thug life."

"In my fuckin' world it is, now chill, you blowin' my high."

"And you blowin' my mind," Penny said as Dru continued shifting his mind again. He took Penny back even further.

"Gotta Rough Neck, Gotta Have a Rough Neck!"

Penny was catching on and grabbed her phone to pull up the lyrics Dru was rapping and she immediately broke his trance again.

"Dru that's fuckin' MC Lyte. God, I love her but why you rappin' all this old shit?" Dru took his index finger and flicked the tip of his nose, another behavior that sprang from somewhere.

"You know just when I think ya ass is catchin' on you crash." Dru quickly swung his body around and hopped up like a child full of energy.

"Wait Dru you're right, I don't get it help my ass turn around off this ledge!" Dru with his gentle hands helped Penny turn around and stand up; with her heels, she almost stood at eye level with Dru.

"There. So, let me help you get it. Music socially develops anyone it's just one tool."

"But why those two songs, Dru?"

"Oh, my bad, they just happened to pop up they fit my world, the only thing is some think it's their world and they ain't even a part of it, and if I'm a rough neck or that's what Black women want me to be, then what happens when I leave my world and go into another part of the world? Or should I say the White world you know what fuckin' happens?"

Penny didn't know if it was the cold wind making her tear up or Dru's piercing words of truth.

"What happens Dru?"

"I become dismantled, get it now it's time to go back through the door. Let's go."

CHAPTER 15

The Antagonist

Dru held Penny's hand as they walked towards the door of the abandoned building. Dru stood for a moment tying a knot in the bag to keep the chicken warm that they never ate. But Dru suddenly stopped and stared at the ground as if he sensed something.

"Dru, what's wrong?"

Dru looked up at Penny but she could tell he was staring at something in the distance. When she turned to look, she saw a young white man standing across the street. Penny noticed that he dressed distinguished with a black dress sweater, tightly fitted black slacks, black dress shoes, and black tinted sunglasses. His blondish hair was slicked back on the sides and spiked at the top. He stood watching Dru and Penny tapping his clove cigarette on his metal case with a smile.

"Dru, do you know him or something?" She could tell before he answered he did because his jaws clenched in anger.

"Yeah, I know his ass!"

"Who is that and why is he smiling like that?"

But Dru opened the abandoned building door and pulled Penny along, and they were back in her apartment.

CHAPTER 16

Working on the Assignment

Dru walked swiftly to Penny's couch kicking his Air Ones off and slinging his Du-Rag to the side. She noticed he was sweating bullets as if he just ran a marathon, but before she could even begin to keep focusing on him, she opened her door back to see her hallway. She shut the door back and turned slowly looking at Dru. He sat with his usual smile and he wasn't sweating anymore. He just sat calmly with his feet crossed on top of the coffee table. Penny folded her arms with a timid look.

"Okay are you gonna explain all this? Why me?"

"Why, not you? Come sit." Penny walked slowly and sat next to Dru.

"Weren't you gonna take your boots off? I know those pretty toes hurt." Penny blushed and did as she was told, then curled up on the couch.

"You say why not me? I'm just an ordinary girl, and obviously I'm not with an ordinary person right now. You are a person, right?"

"Of course, I'm sitting here, right? What you think I'm an alien?"

"No, not at all."

"Too bad you can't tell anybody, not even Tiff and Ebony huh?"

"You're really getting a kick out of this and you're right, I'll be put into a straitjacket if I told anyone what happened to me today."

"Consider yourself a lucky girl."

"So, who was that guy?"

"You'll learn later fuckin' asshole."

"Dru, so they're others like you?"

"Of course, consider yourself a lucky girl."

"Why'd you say he's an asshole?"

"Let's stick to the assignment for now. There are special doors for him now it's my bedtime. Get some rest, we have a big day tomorrow, get cha pretty ass up so I can pull the couch out."

It was the same routine as the night before. Dru slipped out of his clothes, down to his Dago T-shirt and boxers, as if Penny wasn't even there.

"Umm, you could say goodnight."

"Yeah, yeah goodnight sweetie," Dru said as he tied his Du-Rag and opened his laptop, putting his earphones in.

"I thought you were going to sleep?"

"I am, just a little tv to put me to sleep now leave me be."

"Damn, well excuse me."

Penny went to her room and sat on the end of her bed with her head in her hands.

"Shit! Who else does this kinda stuff happen to?" Penny's phone rang and it was Tiffany calling, and for the first time, she didn't pick up.

Penny slipped out of her jeans and slipped into some biking shorts and a T-shirt and couldn't help but to open the door and take a peek at Dru. She saw once again it didn't take him long to fall but his laptop was still on and out of curiosity, she tip-toed to see what he was watching. Penny saw that his earphones were still in but when she looked at the screen, four tv programs played at the same time, each one in the corner of the screen. Penny picked the laptop up to get a closer look.

"Oh wow!" she thought.

In the top left, The Cosby Show played, on the top right The Brady Bunch played, on the bottom left Good Times, and on the bottom right The Partridge Family. Penny looked over at Dru. He slept like a baby and it was as if he had a smile on his face.

Penny looked back at the tv shows, *"Did he do this on purpose? One show is from the 80s, well I guess Good Times is the early 80s and two shows from the late 70s, I think? Now why in the hell would a twenty-five-year-old in 2016 be watching this?"*

Penny took one last look and wondered was he older than what he told her. Penny left the tv program on. She didn't want to wake him by turning them off. Penny tucked under her covers, and the only one she wanted to talk to and might not think she was crazy was her mother. Penny waited patiently at her mother's Billy Joel ringtone.

"Hi honey," Penny's mom answered. No matter what time it was she always answered with her same cheerful voice.

"Hey mom, you got time?"

"Always Honey, now what's wrong? You sound down."

"Sort of. I gotta question."

"And what's that?"

"Don't tell Dad, promise?"

"Hmm, is it about your friend you told me about? Is he alright?"

"Yeah mom, he's fine. But I wanna ask you something else."

"Okay, I'm all ears."

"Do you believe in angels?"

"Whew! That's a heavy question, but a good nine o'clock at night question."

Penny sighed in frustration, "Mom, I'm serious."

"God, I don't know, but I guess so. I don't know how you would recognize one. What made you ask that?"

"Oh nothing, Mom..."

"Well, how's your project coming along?" Penny's eyes rolled to the ceiling.

"Mom trust me, you wouldn't believe me if I told you."

"Oh, it must be interesting."

"Interesting ain't the word, trust me, but Imma let you go now."

"Okay Honey, you call me back if you wanna talk. Now gimme some sugar."

"Muah! Love you Mom."

"Love you too."

The only thing Penny could do before she went to bed was to accept without a doubt that it was a spiritual world and it sure had a puzzling way of presenting itself. From that point on, Dru was an angel to her and she wasn't going anywhere no time soon.

Penny raised up in a panic the next morning from the classic, "Lovely Day" by Bill Withers blasting through the speakers.

"Now what the hell does he got goin' on?" Penny glanced at the clock to see it was 8:30 a.m.

"Oh, he done lost his god-damn mind!"

When Penny went to her living room, she could see the same TV shows were playing on his laptop, a cigarette still burning and Dru dancing in front of the stove. Penny stormed to her stereo and cut the music off.

"Dru!"

"Oh! It's about time you came out ya beauty sleep; breakfast is on the way."

"Dru its 8:30! Why are you having a damn party by yourself?"

Dru quickly turned with two full plates of pancakes, bacon, eggs, and hash brown. She couldn't stay mad too long. Even though it was her food, at least he had the common courtesy to make her a plate.

"Okay, come on eat up, it's a big day," Dru said.

"Are you like this every morning?"

"Sometimes."

"So, what's with your TV shows?"

Penny decided to sit Indian style while she ate. She tried to examine the shows but couldn't tell what was so funny because Dru was having the time of his life.

"Dru, these are some old shows..."

"Shhh, this is hilarious!"

"What's hilarious?"

"Oh, you wouldn't understand, you're mixed." Penny's head jerked back simply because Dru said it so arrogantly.

"Oh, so now I'm mixed. And what do you mean I wouldn't understand?"

"Yeah, you're Black, but you're still mixed damn, what a tragedy."

"What tragedy, Dru?"

"Damn, I gotta explain everything to you."

"Yeah, well maybe you do, Mr. Angel!" Dru looked over at Penny raising one eyebrow.

"Hmm if that's what you wanna call me. Now don't cha see the social development of the Black family?"

"Dru you know what?"

"What Sweetie?" Dru said lightly tapping Penny's thigh.

She wanted to snap at him but she froze again. She could never get used to being called Sweetie and his touch was so gentle.

"I was just gonna say, it seems like you're more into my assignment than me."

"Well, aren't I?"

"So why are those TV shows a tragedy?"

"Well, ya see if I'm having Good Times, I'm doomed, and even when I have moved on up." And suddenly Dru sung the rest of the song to the Jefferson's, clapping his hands.

"Yes, moving on up to a deluxe apartment in the sky! Into Cosby's world, I'm still doomed." Penny shook her head because her newfound friend had a personality she has never encountered. He was a real character.

"Okay Dru, doomed from what?"

"I can't wait to hear this one," Penny thought. Dru raised up quickly as if he just solved a murder mystery.

"Fa crying out loud! The fucking Partridge family can move up and shit is good! But what if you moved fuckin' Michael to the Cosby family that lives in the suburbs? Do you know what would happen?"

"No Dru, what would happen?"

"A catastrophe!" Dru said pounding his fist on his forehead. Penny could see that however Dru saw things, she had to tighten up.

"Okay Dru slow down. A catastrophe?"

"Yes! The Cosby family and others alike would dismantle him."

"And how's that?"

"He's simply gonna run into a bunch of White Cosby families." Penny didn't take that comment lightly.

"Now Dru, that was real bias and narrow minded and you know it."

"Oh! The true words of someone who can choose both sides of the fence at will."

"I could just slap his ass!"

"And what's that supposed to mean? I think both shows were good," Penny said.

"Oh bullshit! The Cosby family ain't nothing but the Brandy Bunch. Once Michael touches base with racism such a tragedy." But Penny wasn't satisfied and decided to challenge Dru.

"Since you know so much than why don't you take me through one of your magical doors and show me."

"So glad you asked. I might be able to arrange that."

"Arrange what?"

"Oh, I have to get permission to go back in time."

"Permission from who?"

"None of your business. That's for me to handle."

"I should have known he was gonna say that," Penny thought rolling her eyes.

"Why back in time?"

"Because it's best to go back to see what was really going on exactly at the time the shows aired."

"I guess that makes sense okay so when do we go?" Penny asked, bouncing up and down as if she was going on a field trip. Dru smiled, getting a kick out of it.

"Easy now pump ya brakes, we'll leave shortly. But first we'll have Good Times. Now go get dressed. And by the way, don't wear those damn high heels again."

CHAPTER 17

Good Times

Penny stood in the mirror holding her hair up and decided to pin it up, throw her sweat suit on and take Dru's advice and wear her Air Max.

"Okay Dru, I'm ready," Penny said and as usual Dru was already fully dressed, sitting patiently.

"Very good, so are you ready?"

"Of course, I see you're dressed pretty simple today no Jesus medallion and Du-rag?"

"Nope! Just my black sweatshirt and jeans will do, plus that other look I mastered that mind already."

"Then why did you dress that way in the first place?"

"For you." Dru took a deep breath as he stood approaching the door.

"I suggest you start taking notes, it's about that time, but now let's go visit another mind."

"Who's mind?"

Dru grabbed Penny's hand just as he did before, raising both eyebrows and Penny's heart pounded. It was still hard to believe something like going to different dimension was happening to her. She even had a part of her mind that still believed she was dreaming.

"Let's go visit Lil Jamal."

Dru opened her door and the door shut. When Penny opened her eyes, she was standing in front of the back doors of an elementary school that led to the playground. Once again Penny looked at Dru placing her hand over her mouth, and Dru folded his arms, chewing his gum with the same smile. Penny looked around the playground, at the kids in the sandbox, some climbing the monkey bars, and some playing a game of kickball.

"Where are we at Dru?"

"Oh, a small suburb. The name isn't needed come on let's go sit in the bleachers," Dru said dragging Penny behind him.

She didn't think she would ever get used to his swift walk but the first thing she noticed was that it definitely wasn't winter, and all the kids had summer clothes on. So Dru did fulfill his promise of taking her back in time. Dru chose to sit at the very top as if he was scanning every child.

"Woah! Dru it's like a damn workout every time I go with you."

Dru laughed slightly, "Sweetheart, you're just time sick."

"Time sick?"

"Yes, not to be confused with seasick I sped your physical composition up in order for you to go backwards."

Penny wasn't a Physics major but there was no such thing as a "dumb question"

"Dru don't you mean slow me down or as you said physical?"

"If I slowed ya atoms down you would dismantle Sweetie but that's a whole lot of mathematics." Penny didn't argue and let it be because what he said was beyond her comprehension.

"Okay so what year is it?"

"1984."

"Are you serious?"

"That's what I said, didn't I?" Dru said obnoxiously, "ah, there he is," Dru said pointing.

"Who?"

"That little boy sitting by himself right there with his chin in the palms of his hands, sitting Indian style."

"Oh, I see, is that Jamal?"

"Yes."

"So why him?"

"Well, he's experiencing Good Times."

"Doesn't look like it. He looks so sad."

"Actually not. His ego has collapsed and now he has to make a choice."

"How old is he? And what choice?"

"Oh, he's about 10 and he won't be returning to the city from which he was born. At least no time soon and I might have to re-word it. He's actually going through a chance of confusion," Dru said lighting his cigarette.

"What's a choice of confusion?"

"Well and take notes, it's a double negative. If he chooses to be with the White kids and I might add, this is a blue collar part, so most of the White kids are what you call 'Poor White Trash' that still of course have a trained thought for being superior or if he chooses the Black kids that have grown up here their whole lives but do not act like the city Black kids he left; so, he sits by himself on the playground remembering the good times; get it?" Penny suddenly jerked back looking at Dru in suspicion.

"Dru, how you know so much about this kid?"

"Well, you asked were there others like me and I agreed, so I'll let you in a little further. Very close associate of mine was assigned to him."

"Assigned? So, you are an angel, I knew it!"

"Not quite love, but if that's what floats your boat but anyway he had to wash his hands of him."

"Oh-My-God, why?"

"Well, Lil Jamal got sucked into the pathological abyss of Whiteness.

Such a tragedy."

"Run that by me again."

"Nope! Told ya to take notes but I will say this, it happens to millions. So, what's your assignment, if you don't mind me asking?"

"Why would I mind?"

"I've already taken you to just a portion of mind pimp and thugs and I could have taken you deeper but not yet. The coffee shop, my collegiate mind, and I could have taken you deeper then and I will, and my assignment," Dru paused blowing smoke to the sky as if he didn't have a care in the world.

"My assignment is much harder."

"And what's that?"

"No worries. Now let's see, what happened to Jamal. Umm, I'll say in six years from now. Shall we?"

Dru took Penny by the hand to the back doors of the elementary school and when they went back through, they entered a high school. It appeared that it was lunch break and high school kids stood in small groups by their lockers.

"Where are we at now?"

"In his most critical years, I would say," Dru said as he pulled Penny in a corner to examine a group of males, four Whites and Jamal.

"Is that him?" Penny pointed. She took a double look at Dru as lit a cigarette. She figured out obviously, no one could see them.

"Yes, he's about 16."

"So, what's the big deal? He looks normal to me."

Jamal stood with his White male friends with his textbooks held tightly close to his chest. His attire was the common prep look. A plaid button-down shirt neatly tucked, jeans, and preppy brown leather thin soled shoes that he purposely wore like the other prep White boys. The back of the shoes smashed down as if they were turned into sandals with no socks.

"Sure, very studious look but he in a deadly dimension and he doesn't know it."

"And what's that?"

"He is in fact in a dimension of color blindness."

"I don't see how."

"Shall we listen to what they're talking about?"

"Sure."

Dru lightly touched Penny's ear with his index finger and her hearing became sharp as a cat. She could hear everything being said as if she were standing with them.

"Pretty neat, huh?" Dru asked.

"So, Jamal, you coming to the Kegger tonight?"

"Fuck yeah, dude!" Jamal said.

"So, do you see?" Dru interrupted.

"Dru, I already know where you're going with this, you're trying to show that he's acting White and I don't agree with that." But as usual Dru boxed Penny in a corner where she couldn't argue.

"Oh really?"

"Yes, really!"

"Actually, you said it first, so if it wasn't true then why did you automatically think that's why I brought you to this point?"

"Because you mentioned color blindness, did you not?"

"Oh, bless your heart, but in this case your definition of color blindness is useless. Yes, indeed he knows he's Black even though he has a fake accent right now. And he knows they're White, however he doesn't realize that every last one of the White males. Oh, and his White girlfriend will turn their back, even destroy him if a certain circumstance ever arisen. So, let's listen some more."

At that moment, a Black girl walked by. Penny did notice that Jamal smiled and laughed at everything the White boys said including, "Hey Jamal, now that's a fat ass, huh bro?" Jamal laughed and his smile widened even more. Dru gently touched Penny ear bringing her hearing back to normal.

"Now, do you see?"

"Yeah, I do that's a fake smile he just gave. I don't know how I know; I just know."

"Now, now don't ever say you don't know. The reason you know because White boys that say such things won't say that in front of certain types of Black men." Penny placed her head down and she couldn't hold it in.

"So, what do you think about my father?" Penny asked folding her arms.

She had the look of a mad jealous wife. But Dru's attention was distracted. He had the same look in his eyes only this time he didn't sweat. Penny turned to see the same distinguished young white man. He was wearing the exact same style of clothes as Jamal and his friends, and he smiled at Dru and winked at Penny.

"Dru there's that guy again."

"Yeah, I know."

Penny watched as the mysterious guy walked over to Jamal, giving him a high five and looking back at Dru and Penny. It was the most devious smile she had ever seen, and he walked off with Jamal with his arms around his shoulders.

"Okay, you gonna tell me who the fuck that is? And the first time you were scared, I remember and now you're cool."

"Who is he?" Penny asked furiously.

"In due time sweetheart. This is your assignment and everything I show you; you must be prepared for." But Penny wasn't having it.

"You know Dru, miss me wit da bullshit!"

"Did you know a little more beauty comes out when you're pissed?" Dru asked as he leaned against the wall.

"Yeah, that's sweet but don't try to distract me! How do you know if I'm prepared or not? Obviously, I've been prepared up to this point! Now who is he? And where's he going with Jamal?"

"Now stop fussin'. We've just got started and like I said, you're not ready. Plus, we have the rest of my mind to cover, remember?"

"Okay, well I wanna put that shit on hold. So, what happens to him?"

"That gentleman, I will explain in due time and actually it's unavoidable, but I will give you this. Jamal is getting ready to start his apprenticeship."

"Huh? His apprenticeship? For what?"

"Well, he could group up to become very educated, get married, have kids and conform to the social order, but and listen to me carefully." Penny looked into Dru's eyes and all the noise in the hallway ceased.

"If the unconscious state of mind of the White man is awakened in his mind and he is not prepared or has no knowledge of it, then it could mean a certain death ultimately." Penny took two steps backwards, and Dru stared with no emotion, tapping his cigarette.

"Why didn't you stop him just now?"

"For one, we're still back in time, and two, Jamal's fate rested in his own hands."

"Rested so this unconscious mind became conscious in his mind?"

"That's correct."

"And what happened?"

"You're a lil hard-headed ass. You know that?"

"Well, I'm a tough hard-headed ass! Now what happened to him?"

"Fine. I'll do this. We'll use two doors," Dru said pointing at the men's restroom and ladies' restroom.

"I'll let you choose, but I won't tell you which door. One door will show you his suicide which he attempted and succeeded. And the other door shows you his mind when the dimension was opened. So, point and choose."

Now that Penny was given full authority over the situation, she felt small as a pea and suddenly wanted to back out but her ego wouldn't let it happen.

"Okay, the men's room."

"That's a good choice. Besides, I don't think you wanna see a man blowin' his brains out, but it's still a bad choice."

"Why?"

"Because what you're about to see, well, you probably would've wished you picked the other door. Come on, let's get it!" Once again, she was being pulled, strung along with force.

"Damn, I think I pissed him off," Penny thought.

This time, she lost her breath from the cold. When she looked back, the door stood alone and she looked around and there were mountains everywhere.

"Dru, it's cold!"

Penny couldn't help but to instantly grab Dru. It was a cold that she never experienced. This cold felt as if it were sucking the life out of her.

"Dru fuck it, let's go, it's too cold."

"No! We won't be here long, go look over that cliff."

Penny walked slowly and the wind slapped her face from both directions. As she got closer, the growls became louder and louder without a doubt she knew she was in a wolf's den. Penny leaned slowly to see the grossest sight. She turned her head in agony but she had to look again. Five white wolves fought each other trying to eat one another. They slung their own flesh and when one died, they duplicated and multiplied faster than her heart could beat.

Suddenly, one wolf looked up at her as if he knew she was there, but the wolf went back to focus on his prey. Dru came up slowly behind Penny.

"I know it's pretty gross." Penny held her stomach trying to keep vomit from coming up.

"Why are they multiplying like that?" Penny asked as she watched the wolves fight and newborn wolves would grow out of their bodies at the same time.

Dru squeezed her shoulder. "Because it appears their eating one another but that's not the case. There fighting for Jamal's mind and he's battling. Come on, we must go now."

CHAPTER 18

Too Deep for Me

Once through the dimensional door, Penny rushed to her couch and curled in a fetal position. The cold she experienced just for a few moments was beyond what she ever could imagine. Dru walked to the thermostat and cranked it to 80 degrees.

"There, the heat is on a little higher. How do you feel?"

"Dru, that was too deep for me."

"Huh, you asked for it, now didn't you?"

"Yeah, but you coulda gave me a damn heads up that shit was too deep."

Dru tilted his head. "Oh well, it should and it will some more but you can handle it." Dru's consoling was suddenly interrupted by a knock at the door.

"Shit. Now who the hell is that?" Penny said as she tip-toed to the door as if it were a bill collector. Penny looked through the peep hole to see it was none other than Tiffany and Ebony.

"Damn it, I forgot Tiff said her ass was gonna show up!"

It wasn't so much that they came unannounced, it was the worry about who Dru really was and she didn't know how he was with other people besides outside the dimensions.

"Knock, Knock! Hello?! It's Tiff and Ebony!"

"Well, you just gonna let their asses sit in the hallway?" Dru asked.

"Shut up, Dru. Course not." Penny opened the door and Tiff and Ebony stormed in as if Penny wasn't even there.

"Girl, you took long enough, it's cold as shit outside; so, this must be your friend," Ebony said.

Penny shut the door and looked at Dru with a pissed look that he knew she was trying to hide.

"Yes, this is Dru. Dru this are my girls, Tiff and Ebony."

"Please to meet you all," Dru said as he shook their hands and Penny watched closely as Dru rubbed his thumbs across the top of their hands.

"He's such a god damn flirt!" Penny said to herself.

She made sure she sat with just enough room for Dru to be close to her. She knew that not so much Tiff, but Ebony was thirstier than a damn bobcat. But she couldn't deny it, even though she knew there was something special about Dru. She still didn't think she was as pretty as them. Both probably could've been models at some point in their lives.

"So, what we doin' tonight?" Ebony asked. Before Penny could answer, Ebony was already on her way to the kitchen.

Tiffany whispered quietly as she could, "girl, I'm sorry but she popped up at my apartment when I was on my way out."

Dru picked up quickly that Tiff was closer to Penny. All eyes were on Ebony as she walked back with four shot glasses. Dru's eyes widened as Ebony switched her hips. She had black leggings, a sports top that showed her belly ring, and short lengthened feather. Before she say she made sure she pulled her leggings up at the waist, as if they were falling down. Something women did to let the man know their ass was big.

"I could just kick her ass!"

"I brought the gin."

"Gin, Ebony? Since when on Sunday night?"

Tiffany had to definitely ask to let Penny know, she definitely didn't know, she brought a pint of Seagram's.

"Umm..." Dru quickly interrupted Penny before she could say no.

"No worries," Dru said as he opened the bottle and poured a shot in each glass. Penny turned slightly folding her arms.

"Oh! So, he thinks I won't kick his ass too!"

Yes, Penny felt the demon of jealousy. It was a situation she always knew about but never faced; a common case of her man being seduced right in her face.

"So Dru, you go to the school?" Ebony asked.

"Now come on doll. You know you already know the answer to that, but since you wanna act like you don't know, no babe, I don't."

Besides him calling her "doll" and "babe," Penny never got use to how Dru responded to things and didn't know how much longer she could watch Ebony's "I wanna fuck you look" and Dru's (or what she suspected) "I wanna fuck you back look." Dru's response went in one ear and out the other, and as usual, a woman's mind shifts like the wind.

"Oh! I forgot to tell y'all, remember that guy..."

Ebony began to rant and rave about the guy in her class, about this and that, shifting on about the latest reality show. Tiffany kept it ladylike and pretended like she was interested. Like Penny, they all grew up together, and they were used to Ebony being the center of attention. Dru leaned back on the sofa. His shoulders were broad. Penny moved slightly but just enough so their shoulders still touched. It was a shoulder kiss.

Dru tuned Ebony out for a second to look at Penny and Penny looked at Dru and bit her bottom lip. She knew Dru kissed her with his shoulder and that was good enough for her. Black women can feel love from the Black man in many different ways, only thing is, the men don't usually they're even doing it.

Dru gave a smirk and Penny began to copy wondering what he was up to. Dru took his index finger and lightly touched her left temple. Penny looked back at Tiff and Ebony, she didn't' wanna be rude even though Ebony hadn't shut up since she came with the gin.

"Damn that bitch talks a lot!" Dru though and Penny jumped because she could hear his thoughts.

"Girl, you okay?" Ebony asked.

"No, I mean, yeah girl, I'm straight."

"Oh, okay but anyway like I was saying, so he take me to this cheap ass restaurant that ain't even in my league."

Penny looked at Dru with both her lips tucked in. She couldn't believe it was surprise after surprise, she could hear everything he was thinking.

"Stop lookin' so surprised, just go with the flow. Ya girls gonna think you crazy," Dru thought and Penny followed suit trying her hardest to hold her laughter in.

"God! This bitch talks like she drinks fuckin' gasoline! Fuck some gin." The shoulder kiss became an elbow punch to Dru.

"Why you do that? She don't know what I'm thinking and I should let you know; you can answer back if you want." Penny cleared her throat; she definitely wasn't a gin drinker.

"So, you can hear me?" Penny thought.

"Umm lightbulb! I just told you that." But Penny got caught by Tiff and Ebony from her second elbow punch to Dru.

"Y'all two okay?" Ebony asked.

"Girl, they straight."

That was the least and the last thing Tiff could say considering she knew Penny was gonna cuss her out later and because Ebony wasn't gonna shut up no time soon.

"But anyway, she he workin' on his master's and you know I'm on my B... so I was like, we so perfect and...

"You know love, this is a real rinky-dink ass bitch you got for a friend? And quit elbow punchin' me."

"Stop that Dru."

"Naw, I'm serious. This chick thinks I give a damn about all her degrees and shit, and she thinks she got all the damn sense." Penny finally got to hear the thoughts of a Black's man mind, so she went with the flow.

"Why you say she think she got all the sense?"

"I'm just saying, it's 15 degrees and this bitch got some damn leggings on and a fuckin' belly top. I know her ass is cold."

"Ain't you a little harsh?"

"And whoever that dude is workin' on his master's, he probably sees right through this reality TV hoe."

"Dru, now stop that!"

"Watch this."

"Excuse me love, you think you can get the orange juice?" Dru asked Ebony and without hesitation she followed suit.

"Now you see that?"

"See what, Dru?"

"That bitch doesn't have a gap. When she came through the door, her thighs was rubbin' and now they as wide as the fuckin' Grand Canyon! She need to cut it out wit the games. Oh, and the tuck slit she made so I could see the pussy lips, I peeped that too!'

Ebony hurried back and Tiff looked oddly at Penny. Dru could hold a straight face and talk through his mind. However, Penny was having a real hard time.

"But Dru, that's the in thing."

"Man, that shit is nasty! Please don't ever ask me to go anywhere wit this loudmouth bitch." Even though everything that Dru thought sounded good to Penny's mind, she still wasn't satisfied; she was still a woman.

"So, would you have sex with her?" Penny thought giving Dru a quick look. The look of "you can't lie now cause I know what you're thinking."

"No! That's a crazy question."

"Why is it crazy?"

"Cuz, I respect my dick." Penny choked on her last sip of gin. She had never heard or thought that Black men thought that way.

"Respect your dick??"

"Of course. The moment I quit respecting my dick aww man! Child support, unwanted kids, STD's and shit! And besides, she really one of those chicks that's lookin' for a prostitute."

"She's not gay and she ain't a pimp."

"I know she's not gay, but she's one of those chicks want a nigga to bunny hop on her pussy all day and control. You know sucka shit."

"How you know all this?"

"Been there and done it. Oh, by the way, that's a nice song you got stuck in ya head." Penny looked at Dru, not so much embarrassed but now it was a dead giveaway about how she felt.

"Yeah, I meant to tell you that about five minutes ago when you went into your music files and played it. You like that song Dru?"

"Now stop it. Mary J, I Can Love You Better Than She Can? Classic."

In the midst of Ebony's conversation, Dru managed to slightly touch Penny's temple and their thought connection was cut.

"So Dru, how old are you?" Tiffany asked hoping she could somehow switch the conversation.

"I'm 25, why do you ask?"

"Just asking, that's all. You from around here?"

"Sort of."

"You must got Indian in ya family," Ebony interrupted.

"Don't we all?"

Dru's keen sense of humor; since Penny knew him best, she could tell that he really was making a joke out of her and she didn't even realize it.

"Well yeah, my great-great grandmother was..."

"Let me guess, Cherokee?"

"Yeah, how'd you know?"

"Because all Black people say that shit." Tiffany choked and cleared her throat.

It was the first time she or Penny ever heard a guy make Ebony shut up. And Dru definitely didn't stop there.

"Yeah, we act like the only damn tribe was the freakin' Cherokee tribe."

"Okay, then name some," Ebony said with a slight attitude.

She quickly picked up that all her flirtatious behavior didn't even matter to Dru.

"Well, you had Cherokee, Navajo, and Blackfoot for example. Oh, and by the way, you only asked me that as a compliment to my hair. Kinda hilarious."

"Okay, you right, but why is it hilarious?"

Ebony gave Dru a sarcastic look and Penny put her head down because she wished she could put her own foot in Ebony's mouth.

"Well, it's hilarious because you're paying homage to the Indians based on my damn waves, when you should be paying homage to the Indians for aiding us in our slave revolts where interbreeding occurred, get it?" Dru explained, but Ebony still didn't stop there.

She really showed and proved she must be a pain freak or in this case, an embarrassment freak.

"You must be a Muslim?"

"Actually, no. But can I ask you a question?" This time Ebony hesitated.

She was so busy asking questions, she definitely wasn't prepared to get asked any.

"Sure, go ahead."

Before Dru asked, he bumped Penny's foot, a signal to let her know she should be paying attention.

"Why is it when a Black man speaks intelligent or knows history, you chicks automatically think he's a Muslim? You all act like Muslims own the words 'intelligence' and 'history'."

Penny started thinking of ways to cut the evening short because she didn't know if it was the gin or Dru, but...

"And by the way, you're gonna make a horrible anthropologist with that type of thinking Ebony. You need to really tighten up."

"You know what? Let me tell ya ass..."

"Woah! Okay, Tiff, Ebony I think it's time to go. Dru and I gotta discuss something."

Penny grabbed Tiff and Ebony and headed them to the door. She definitely whispered in Tiff's ear about how she was gonna cuss her out.

CHAPTER 19

The Assignment

Penny slammed the door and looked at Dru with disgust. She didn't even know if she should have been mad at him or not.

"Well, we might as well finish the gin. Plus, you've got one more vacation day."

"Dru! Now why did you talk to her like that?"

"Didn't mean too, now come sit and stop fussin'." And that she did, but she couldn't help but to burst into her realm of nosiness.

"So, when were you gonna let me know you know how to do that?"

"Do what?" Dru asked blowing small smoke rings in the air.

"You know we could talk to each other with our minds."

"I don't have to tell you everything. Plus, that would take the fun out of the assignments."

"I knew it, you are on assignment. You are an angel, right?"

"If that's what you wanna call me."

"I hate when he does that shit," Penny thought as she curled up on the couch, but this time, she sat completely on the opposite end.

"I guess I have to tell you, nobody at least that I've seen, ever made that girl shut up and I've known her since forever."

"Yeah, ya girl, like most, she's been fed and beautifully groomed into nonsense."

"Why do you say nonsense?"

"Put it this way love, nonsense can be used as a deadly weapon and once a person is taken over by it, they have become pathological."

Penny was no psychiatrist but the more Dru revealed, she began to understand his assignment, but she, for some reason or another, knew not to call him out on it.

"You know what I wanna ask next."

"Sure, go ahead."

"The wolves. You said he's in a battle."

"Yes, I hate to classify all but I'm allowed to guess and probably 90% of Black men go through it, usually when they tell, they get fed a bunch of psycho-babble bullshit that usually ends with them taking pills and shit."

"Yeah, but when does it start?"

"Good question, all I can tell you is they might see or hear something or illicit drugs can open the dimensions to the wolves."

"So, how many dimensions are there?"

Dru folded his hands, "I like to call 'em mind-states and we have a long walk, and right now, it's about that time, so it's my bedtime and I know you have to call Tiff, don't you?"

"You such an ol' man you go to bed so early and how do you know I'm a call Tiff?"

"Because you're closer to her and she definitely didn't mean to bring that misguided ass sista with. So, go get some rest. I have to prepare my mind for our walk tomorrow." Penny did as Dru wished and went to bed.

An hour had passed and as she took reflection notes in her notebook, she couldn't help but wonder if this would be an ordinary assignment and what she'd gotten herself into. Even though Penny planned to call Tiff, her best friend beat her to the punch.

"Hey girl, I know you gonna cuss me out."

"Girl, why did you bring her loudmouth ass? You know how she is."

"She popped up and just invited herself. Shit, what was I supposed to say?"

"Tiff, I ain't even worried bout that. I wanna ask you a question."

"How you doin' with this assignment for Professor Brooks?"

"Oh, I forgot to tell you. I'm asking my uncle and he is a trip. He one of them ol' skool men still stuck in the 80s, girl. He's a trip." Penny quickly reflected to when Dru took her on the west side, "I mean, I really wanna ask how many personalities does a Black man have?"

"Shit, I never really thought about it. Why you ask?"

"Okay, do you think someone or a Black man can have multiple personalities? You know like one day he's a pimp and the next day, he's a thug?"

"Okay, it's a difference. Is he actually living it?"

"Yes, but let's say he knew how to live out all personalities or behaviors no matter how many." Tiffany had no idea that Penny was completely serious and laughed.

"All I can tell ya if it's a Black man doin that it's either one or the other."

"What's that?"

"Shit, he either Superman or he crazy."

"Okay Tiff, I'm a let you go, call me later."

Penny just like anyone else loved the Superman example Tiffany gave, but she was still convinced that Dru was an angel, and the last thing she wouldn't want to believe.

"Would God make a crazy angel and if so, what the hell was his purpose?"

But that question didn't last long, simply because crazy people didn't know they were crazy. The only thing she did know was that Dru was taking her through stages and it had to be for a deeper purpose.

Penny took notes for as long as she could and dozed off but was suddenly awakened. The clock showed 1:00 a.m., but it felt like she was only asleep for 10 minutes. She could hear someone talking in the living room so she listened for a moment to the unusual speech. Unusual only because of the hour and once again, she was preparing to kick his ass.

"Oh, hell no, I know his ass ain't watchin' a damn porno in my fuckin' living room!"

Penny threw her covers back and as she got closer to her door; she couldn't even open it right away because it was Dru's voice.

"Oh Yeah! Yeah, Yeah, you fuckin' a real nigga! Now hike dat ass up."

They say when people talk in their sleep, supposedly that's what they truly desired. Penny wondered as for the dream Dru was having what he truly desired. Temptation caressed her inner thighs as she got wet instantly and fought the urge to slip under the covers with him and make his dream complete. But the doubt of another woman and Penny not being Dru's dream girl would've been a huge embarrassment so she just sat back and listened. Penny felt like a peeping tom but listened as he repeated the same words over again.

"Yeah! Yeah! You fuckin' a real nigga now."

Out of lust, she was turned on. 'Hmm? Fuckin' a real nigga?' Penny went back in her room and jotted down in her notes exactly what he said, word for word, and the only questions that remained were, *"What the hell is a real nigga? and why was I turned on by it?"*

CHAPTER 20

Cougar

The smell from the hot cup of cocoa that on Penny's nightstand when she awakened made her really believe that it was her that Dru dreamt of. Why else would he make cocoa for her first thing in the morning?

"Wow, that's so sweet of him." Penny saw a small note next to the cup.

Good morning Ms. Penny,

I hope you enjoy the cocoa. At exactly 11:45 a.m., leave your apartment. Don't worry about where you're going, just follow the instructions. 11:45 exactly.

Penny looked over at the clock. It was 11:30 a.m. and she still didn't quite understand that Dru was already gone. Penny rushed into the living room and the pull-out couch was neatly put back together, and she noticed the three duffle bags were in the corner, but she didn't have time to worry about that. She only13 minutes to get ready. Whatever or wherever Dru was leading her to, she remembered he had to prepare his mind, whatever the case it couldn't be as bad as where he'd taken her the night before. Penny stood patiently holding the doorknob.

"I can't believe I'm doing this."

It was 11:44 a.m., and just like a child would do, she couldn't wait, and open the door to find the empty hallway.

"Okay close the door, you only got 10 seconds."

Penny counted the seconds down while her heart pounded with each second. Three, two, one! Penny opened her door slowly and saw she was in a penthouse living room. She moved slowly to the balcony windows that overlooked the lakefront. The penthouse was immaculate. She sat patiently on the leather sofa. A pack of Newport's and a 24oz can of 211 sat on the cocktail table, sit it was obvious that Dru was nearby. 'Now why would he bring me here?'

But one thing she knew for certain was that this was a woman's house by the light perfume smell and her sense of style was on point. She heard a woman's voice coming from the bedroom.

"You so silly."

She could hear Dru laughing as if he was having the time of his life. Penny's heart sunk and the only thing she could think was that he was playing a hurtful joke.

"He knows that I like him. He did this shit on purpose," Penny though to herself as tears ran down her face, but she at least wanted to see the woman.

She saw down the hallway that the bedroom door was about an inch open, so she took a deep breath and wiped her tears. The closer she got to the door, the laughter made her tears return, and she thought to herself that *he must not be single after all.* She peeped through the cracked door and had a clear view of Dru on his back as his mistress straddled on top. There was no question about it.

"His fuckin' Juggalo ass!" Penny thought as she looked to see that his mistress was every bit of fifty.

"Dru, you so silly. You always keep me laughin'," the woman said.

Penny couldn't deny it. The woman was beautiful with a body of a 20-year-old and as bad as she wanted to storm in, her hurt wouldn't allow it.

"Well, lil mama, it's time for me to go, you know I got shit to do," Dru said.

"You always do that, baby I told you, you can move in."

"This old ass bitch fuckin' roses tattooed above her ass!" Penny thought.

"My bad lil mama what? You want me to beat that pussy up again?"

"Oh, I'm definitely not gonna watch this shit!"

Penny sat on her couch staring at her front door like a wife awaiting a husband that's been out with the fellas all night. Her mind raced from thought to thought.

"Now I see where the hell he gets his money from. Why is he homeless? He doesn't even have to be. I wonder how old her ass is?"

Her trance suddenly stopped as Dru came through the door. He gave his usual half devious smile.

"So, you think that's real fuckin' funny?" Penny said.

Her nostrils flared since he had this attitude as if he were surprised, she was even mad. Dru calmly sat on the couch, kicked his feet up on the coffee table, and counted out a few hundred-dollar bills. He had so many clothes, she couldn't tell if he already had new Jordan's or if his mistress bought them. Penny couldn't help but slap him on his shoulder.

"Answer me Dru! That was some real bullshit! You know what, let me see this damn wallet!"

Dru didn't resist; he just sat and watched as Penny took out a couple more hundreds.

"What are you looking for sweetheart?"

"Don't call me sweetheart and where's you ID? I'm sick of this in the dark shit!"

"Oh, you finally decided to ask to see an ID after all this time. Well, I don't need an ID, it's not needed for my assignment, and why are you so mad?" Dru said with no emotion which pissed Penny off even more.

"Why am I pissed? How old is she? And what was the point of all that shit?! And I heard you talkin' in ya sleep ya lil perverted ass dream..."

"Easy now easy."

"Don't tell me to be easy." Dru lightly poked Penny's shoulder with his index finger.

"You're not paying attention. I told you ya girl just wants a nigga to bunny hop on the pussy all day, remember?"

"I don't get..."

"Yeah, I know, you never do but let me help you out... that's how ya girl is gonna end up. I had to take you into the cougar and the prostitute dimensions."

"Okay, explain and this better be good cuz you really need to cover your ass right now." Penny knew that statement was useless and Dru was too keen and slick.

"Well, sweetheart and I'm not gonna say all, but ya girl or I should my cougar all her relationships are gonna go up in flames. She's gonna grow old and lonely and look for really young Black men to bunny hop on the pussy when she feels like it, buy me Jordan's, keep the Newport's, and whatever other vice I have here on location, and keep bread in my pocket. The cougar is just what she is, but it's prostitution for her prey. It's just another deadly honeycomb state-of-mind hideout. Now did that make sense?" And it did, once again Dru had boxed Penny into a corner.

"Dru all that makes sense but do you enjoy living like that?"

"Told you, I'm on assignment, but for your assignment, you might wanna make note that if I choose to remain in that state-of-mind than brothaz already know they have to remain going in circles for the rest of their lives.

"What do you mean going in circles, Dru?" Penny took a deep breath because everything that came out Dru mouth always seemed to make her shake her head.

"Well, in his mind, he thinks he's advancing but he's just movin' in a circle. He knows he's just a bitch's pet."

"Dru you're making this really hard."

"The circular part is, I gotta cougar in Roger's Park, where you were at..." Penny's eyes widened.

"A cougar in Hyde Park, she's got a 401K, a cougar in Evanston, teaches at Northwestern, and a White cougar in Oak Brook."

"Dru, I don't believe that." But deep down, Penny knew he was telling the truth by the next question he asked as he winked his eye.

"Penny who do you think gave older Black women the title cougar? Women don't like to address their age, period! Especially when their over 40 so cut and dry. A Black cougar with a man her age is no longer a cougar, so a cougar is a woman looking to prostitute a younger man. Basically, I would never become a man with four cougars I don't have to work a day of my life."

Penny stared for a moment watching Dru blow circles of smoke in the air, it was if he was hypnotized with the circles, and he took his index finger and broke one.

"Dru, how does he break out of that state of mind?"

"Good question, he has to confront something and no matter how small or big the circle, he can't run in the circle forever."

"What's the something he has to confront?"

"It'll be part of our walk. Be patient."

"And your dream? What does fuckin' a real nigga mean?"

"I sense some jealousy in your voice but to answer your question, that's the invisible measuring rod he never wants to believe that he's really nothing more than a dick to the financially stable cougar."

CHAPTER 21

Pathology Mathematics

Mind racing in a deep daydream again, Penny sat in Professor Brook's lecture and all she could see was his lips moving. No matter how hard she tried, she just couldn't believe her first romantic crush turned out to be with an angel of some sort. She giggled to herself off the fact that he just moved himself in.

"I still can't figure out what he's trying to show me. If he didn't have these powers, he'd definitely be a psychopath. I wonder how many more mind-states does he has? I guess all of this will come together eventually."

"Excuse me, Ms. Hampton!" Professor Brooks shouted. All eyes were suddenly on Penny.

"Yes, Professor, I'm sorry."

"Would you like to share with the rest of the class what you're daydreaming about during my lecture?" But Penny was saved by something, thoughts came to her mind that were beyond her control.

"Well actually, I would love to sir."

Professor Brooks tilted his head to the side, as if Penny was making a joke out of his question.

"Then I think we all would like to hear what your daydream is about."

"Well sir, since I've began the assignment, I've found through my client that predominately, most of the external influences that play a part in the social development of African American men is a term I've coined "Pathology Mathematics.""

"Pathology Mathematics?"

"Yes Sir, it is a system of operative pathological behavior that African American men have acquired due to racism in America."

At once, one of the most feared professors on campus had become the student.

"So, Ms. Hampton I see you've gotten to the study of pathology with the individual who you've chosen for your assignment?"

"Well sir, I must add on to the fact that if an oppressor is the pathologist, then the dictionary's definition which you just used is totally useless."

"Explain."

"It's useless because if the oppressor is the pathologist, it take on a different meaning, in other words, that person is the greater influence of all pathological disorders in African American men."

"Oh, I see," Professor Brooks said an odd look of defeat.

Professor Brooks continued with his lecture and Penny saw that even some of her classmates were copying exactly what she said. She had no idea who was speaking through her but she did take a wild guess that Dru had something to do with it.

Class ended shortly and Penny tried her hardest to be the first one out the door. She had a feeling Professor Brooks wasn't done with her.

"Penny, I'd like for you to stay behind for a moment."

Penny went back to her seat, trying to ignore the smiles from the other classmates. Professor Brooks was in his late fifties and had been teaching at the campus for 15 years. He was a Black man with a strict constitution for education. Penny had often wondered did he even have a sense of humor, but for the first time she saw him give a half smile as he leaned back in his chair.

"Penny, pull up a chair."

Penny walked eagerly towards his desk. She felt like she had made history. The rumor was that no student had ever talked to Professor Brooks for more than five minutes. His total work ethic was strictly class and exams, that's it, and that's all. Most of her exams were either pass or fail. Penny sat in front of him staring at his snow-white hair and her smile left as soon as his did.

"Shit, I knew he was a sour puss.'

"Penny first, I would like to say it's not so often that I get a student with such an unusual insight."

"Thank you, Professor."

"That was not a compliment."

"Oh, I..."

"Penny that's a challenge and I am humored to have a student that is challenging usual insight but I have one question does the individual that you're studying have anything to do with your coined term which would still be considered theory?" Penny became extremely nervous and any loss of eye contact would've clearly showed she might not know what she was talking about.

"Well, yes Sir, he actually does."

"Then you have two thumbs up from me and I'm very interested to see how your final assessment turns out," Professor Brooks paused before continuing, "hmm pathology mathematics, very ear catchy." Even though she still didn't know where her newfound term came from, she couldn't believe she won Professor Brooks over.

"Thank you so much, and I can assure you..."

"Penny, I said ear catchy for a reason we must be careful your brief definition of pathology mathematics is serious stuff and cannot be dealt with lightly. Now, I'll see you next class session."

CHAPTER 22

A Heart is Never Done

"You are doing dine. Each dimension you've taken her to, I've weighed your heart and you've been sincere. However, you are still not done!"

CHAPTER 23

Infection

Penny could smell Dru's coffee in her hallway even before she reached her door. It was another bitter cold day in Chicago and no matter what Dru said she didn't feel like doing anything that had to do with her assignment. Penny silently stuck her in key in the door. She hadn't even become aware that it was like she was sneaking in her own house. Her adrenaline rushed as she opened the door. She didn't know what to expect out of Dru. Penny gave a genuine smile, looking at Dru type away on his laptop, wondering what the Hell he was up to now.

Penny noticed his plaid Polo hat, designer glasses that he had on the top of his nose, a wool Polo teddy bear sweater, freshly creased jeans, and pearly white Rod Laver tennis shoes.

"I wish he'd stay one way for Christ's sake."

"So, you just gonna stand there shaking your head?" Dru asked.

"No, I'm just admiring your look today those are some expensive clothes. Oh, I forgot, you got cougars."

"Nice joke, and no my cougars didn't buy any of these clothes. So how was class?"

"I don't know, why don't you tell me Mr. Pathology Mathematics."

Dru took a sip of his coffee and Penny's face frowned. She still couldn't understand how people drank straight black coffee.

"I see you got my thought message."

"Yes, I did sir. You could've at least warned me."

"For what you need to stop daydreaming in class anyway."

Her immediate thought was to pick an argument. Deep down inside, Dru's sarcasm still turned her on.

"So, how often do you snoop around in my mind?"

"Not often love. I do respect privacy rights."

"What are you typing?" Penny asked, trying to read the screen, but her attention was shifted by Dru's watch.

"Where the Hell did you get a Rolex watch from?!" Penny grabbed Dru's wrist.

The closest she has ever been to a Rolex was window shopping. Dru was gentle and pried Penny's beautiful, manicured nails that nearly dug in his skin and placed them on her legs.

"Easy hun, I might get cha one if you have behave."

Penny signed, rolling her eyes. "Oh, stop it with the games, and what the hell are you typing?"

"You're so nosy but for your information, I'm putting funds in my offshore account."

"Huh?"

"Huh what?"

"Let me guess, this is part of the assignment?"

Dru looked up slowly. His eyes widened as he pushed his glasses on his face. He leaned towards Penny's face.

"Definitely is. White collar crime now let's go!"

Penny's mouth hung open and Dru was out the door along with his laptop. He didn't shut the door and Penny found her forehead inside the palms of her hands once more.

"Fuck, here we go again! Dru wait!"

Penny went through the door and Dru moved her to the side and locked the door. She forced herself to swallow as she stared at the .45 caliber on the bed of the hotel room, she was in. There were four credit card machines and credit cards scattered all over.

"Dru what the fuck is this?"

"Calm down baby. I got this," Dru said. Penny had never seen him so cool and calm, but she felt like she was having a nervous breakdown.

She saw everything from Visa to American Express. She picked one of the cards up examining the name.

"Dru you are going to fucking jail! Oh my God!"

"Gotta beat the system, ya feel me. It's all gravy." Dru's slick smile made Penny panic even more.

"Dru! I know one goddamn thing white collar crime, black collar, purple, or yellow, yo ass is going to jail and I..."

"Quit buggin' love, you should be proud," Dru said as he lit a Black & Mild.

"Proud! Proud! Proud of what?!"

"Shit boo gotta get past those flunky ass niggas still selling crack." But that response definitely didn't call Penny down.

"Dru let me tell you something. Crime is fucking crime!" She noticed everything she said went out the window.

Dru swiped a credit card and tossed one to the side.

"There's 40 racks boo! Easy money," Dru laughed when she fell back on the bed because that figure took the life out of her.

"Dru! Forty thousand, you just stole forty thousand! Oh, my God, I am going to fucking jail! And stop laughing at me!"

"Sorry sweetheart, but I'm an angel remember? So, no worries."

"Okay, I forgot. But I'm not a damn angel and my ass is gonna end up in jail!"

Dru sat down slowly next to Penny. He gently poked her thigh with his index finger and all her anxiety went away.

"Experience is the best teacher. The revelation of this dimension is that you gave yourself the answer. I just showed you."

"What answer?"

"You said it best. White, Black, Purple, or Yellow-crime is crime."

Penny was still puzzled for what did that have to do with her assignment.

"Okay, and?"

"And somewhere along the way, Black men today find themselves in the illusion that they're really classes when it comes to crime. The opposite of white is black, so you have some that purposely do certain crimes just to make it to the Feds. Interesting, isn't it? There are actually some that believe they're better than other Black men who sell crack for example."

"Dru, I'll see you back in the living room. We need to talk." Dru sat for a moment watching Penny shoot back through the door.

"Hmmm, well that went well I guess it is time for a talk."

Dru watched as Penny closed all her blinds as if they were having a secret meeting and he sat in his normal spot on the couch. He smiled and Penny raced in the kitchen, grabbed a Heineken, and she was back quick fast sitting on the couch, Indian style.

"Okay, number one, you're gonna start talking and take that sarcastic ass smile off your face."

"So sorry, sweetheart would you like some gum?"

"No, I don't want no damn gum."

"Okay, so what do you want to talk about?"

"Are you going to be honest?"

"I'm always honest, I just reveal when the time is right. And right now, I don't think I have a choice in the matter. Because you definitely look like someone pissed in your cornflakes this morning."

"And he's right he pisses me off because I can't even stay mad at him," Penny thought to herself.

No matter how Dru responded, he responded to seriousness with a sense of humor.

"Okay, who are you and I want straight answers!"

"Yo, flexin' ass, but I like how serious you're trying to sound."

"Shut up! I am serious."

"Okay, I'm a minor God."

"What the Hell is that?"

"You asked for a straightforward answer. God, I'm glad I'm not on assignment for the black woman. You all never can make up your minds."

"Oh, really? Look who's talking and give me a piece of gum."

"You see, I just offered ya ass a piece of gum."

"Okay, well, I want a piece now."

"Sure. I'm real stingy with the Juicy Fruit. So, here's a piece and don't make this a habitual thing."

Penny found herself again trying not to laugh. She was starting to realize that she might be as silly as Dru was in some aspects.

"So, when were you born and where?"

"Right here in the Windy City."

"Don't avoid the other question."

Penny had never saw Dru give a full smile and she could tell that the year he was about to give definitely wasn't going to add up to his physical age.

"1916 honey."

Penny choked on a small sip of beer. Drew actually said the year on purpose while she sipped just to see her reaction.

"You're a hundred?"

"Absolutely, growing old so gracefully. Don't cha think?"

"But your body..."

"Yeah, I know too sexy."

"Shut up Dru, I was going to say you're only twenty-five."

"Damn, you can't add the sexy?"

"Okay, Dru, yes for crying out loud, yes you're sexy."

"God, he's so damn arrogant, he knows he's sexy as shit."

"Why thank you, slide the ashtray."

"So, what's your assignment?"

"Aren't you going to ask how long I'm going to live?"

"Okay, how long?"

"Until my assignment is complete."

"So forever?"

"One hundred and twenty-five years is a pretty shitty deal. One of my close associates is at the 125 mark or year."

"One hundred and twenty-five year?! So, there's more of you?"

"Yes, millions, and he is a she."

"She's a girl?"

"Sure, my home girl Too Short."

"Too Short??? That's her name?"

"Sure, she's really going through it right now."

"Through what?"

"Well love at a certain point, we have to check out of society it's pretty hard to do."

"Why?" Dru folded his hands across his chest.

"We have to check out of society in order to see the bigger picture."

"But you..."

"Yeah, I know. You saw me engage with my pimp homies and this might seem confusing, but I'm part of certain mind states of Black man because I'm on assignment and at the same time I'm not."

"So why is Too Short going through it?"

"Well, we all have different assignments that are all geared toward one objective. I have to command her."

"Why?"

"Because she's a mixture and she adds up to a Puerto Rican, and right now as we speak, she's trying to find a formula to keep the Hispanic community from committing assault on the Black community, lots of politics in this shit."

"So, let me get this straight, nobody recognizes that you never get old?"

"Penny when are enslaved and trapped within nonsense especially in 2016, they don't even recognize the most obvious shit. Get it?" As confusing as it sounded Penny was being introduced into the spiritual realm.

"So are you gonna get to what your assignment is. Please." Dru still got a kick out of Penny's curiosity.

"I'll give you a little bit and don't beg because if I tell you everything, it'll make your assignment less interesting."

"Okay, I promise I won't ask anymore."

"Basically, I have to infect myself with every acquired personality the

Blackman has in this part of the world."

"Oh, I get it, so you're like a spy?"

"No, doll face, I'm not a spy. In order to solve the problem, I have to infect myself with it, and that's highly dangerous." Penny had a quick reflection from their first date.

"So, you said on our first date you was on your talented tenth shit, that's Dubois terminology."

"Just because I go into the mind-state doesn't mean I accept it, but Dubois he was a pretty sharp cat, but his ass was wrong." Penny covered her mouth trying to hide her smile because she has never heard anyone say such a thing.

"Dru, now stop that you don't have to say it like that, but what was he wrong about?"

"Well, sweety, you don't classify some middle-class bourgeois Blacks in college as the saviors of the Black race. Oops! That shit didn't work." Penny slapped Dru's shoulder.

"Dru stop that!"

"I'm just keepin' it real and besides the talented tenth are somewhere else but I understand his plight. Education is necessary but his talented tenth definitely aren't in college classrooms."

"Where are they at?"

"Now stop begging, we'll visit that along the way. Remember our walk isn't done."

"So why..."

"You know love, if you would just shut up and walk the walk with me, you might not have to keep asking why, why, why. Get it?"

"You make me sick."

"I know, so what."

"Okay but can we make one rule?"

"And what's that?"

"Can you at least give me a heads up before you change into who or whatever?"

"Absolutely not, that would take the experience out of it. Now fix something to eat. We need to get rest; you don't have class tomorrow and it's a big day."

"That's it, so you just gonna leave me hangin'?"

"Pretty much now go call Tiffany or something."

Going to bed wasn't as easy for Penny as it was for Dru, and I was the same routine, as soon as he laid down, he was sound asleep, so why not call Tiffany.

"What's up, sis?" Tiffany answered.

"Nothing much girl, just giving you my daily call. What's up with Ebony?"

"Talked to her earlier. I think she's still in recovery from her encounter with your boyfriend..."

"Stop it girl, he's not my boyfriend."

"And let me guess he's still there."

"And yes, he is." Penny could tell by the way Tiffany took a deep breath she really didn't approve.

"Okay, whatever floats your boat, but let me tell you about my damn uncle. I told you I picked him four our assignment."

"Yeah, what happened?"

"Okay, you know he is stuck in pimp world?" Penny couldn't help but laugh when she reflected on E-Money.

"So, what happened?"

"He picks me up so we can go out to eat and his ass comes out with big ass fur hat and some damn beaver fur around his neck!"

"Oh Wow!"

"Wow, ain't the word! I thought it was a damn possum! So, I ask him what the Hell is that?"

"What he say?"

"Oh, ya see lil niece, this shit 100% beaver, go ahead and feel. You there?"

"Yes girl, I'm here. You just got me crying laughing right now."

"So, where did y'all go eat, if you don't mind me asking?"

"You think this shit is real funny. We went to the damn Olive Garden! I wish you could've seen the expression on the waitresses faces. I'm like please don't let this lady ask what is that?" Penny put her head under the covers, hoping she didn't wake Dru. She hadn't laughed so hard in all her life.

"And then guess what?"

"Oh God, what Tiff?"

"She did ask!"

"I'm like now his head getting ready to get in the clouds again."

"How he say it again?"

"I see this is just ticklin' the shit outta you."

He looks and says, "Ya see baby girl, this 100% bizzeava, ya feel me?""

"Oh Lord."

"But it gets better. After she leaves, he gets a call and puts the shit on speakerphone, right."

"Okay and..."

"And it's some boy. He could've been more than seventeen by the sound of his voice and he's talking like my damn uncle!"

"Are you serious?"

"Yeah, so I ask him, so who was that? And he tells me it's his apprentice and he gotta pass the crown down."

"Girl, you wore me out with that one!"

"My bad, but I couldn't wait to tell you that scenario, but enough about me. So, what's Dru like in your study?"

Penny became very quiet. She definitely didn't expect Tiff to ask about Dru and she definitely didn't know where to begin.

"Umm it's going alright."

"Okay I'm a take umm for an answer and I'll give you a call tomorrow. Cool?"

"Cool, love ya sis."

CHAPTER 24

Divine Dreams

Unfortunately, Penny didn't wake up feeling too well. A scratchy throat and stuffed nose was a clear sign she had caught a cold. It was 10:45 a.m. and all Penny could think about was a hot cup of fruit blended tea and of course, Dru. Two cups sat next to Dru on the coffee table. Penny was still in her black leggings and a t-shirt while Dru was fully dressed.

"Well, good morning," Dru said watching Penny stumble onto the couch.

"I feel like shit Dru."

"I know you're sick. There's some tea." Penny noticed Dru was dressed very simple, a pair of jeans, tennis shoes, and a black sweatshirt.

"I see you're not wearing nothing that flash today, and how'd you know I was sick?"

"Cuz, I just know, and since you are, I decided to lay you in."

"That's so considerate of you," Penny sarcastically smacked her lips and rolled her eyes; she noticed Dru staring at her thighs.

Most looked at women in tight leggings and they were usually sexually aroused, but that wouldn't be the case with Dru. He simply rose up from the couch. His face was pleasant and gentle. What better time and place, a warm cozy living room, hot sex on a cold winter morning.

"Oh God, he's finally going to take me," Penny thought and what a good thought it was for the moment.

Because Dru definitely didn't fulfill it. He simply turned around, popped his feet on the other end of the couch and laid his head on Penny's lap.

Penny's hot sex thought left, and a short reflection came to her mind from when she had her first mother daughter talk. Penny envisioned her mother saying, *"Always remember sex too early will destroy a greater more everlasting love."* Penny came out her little trance to see Dru placed his earbuds in.

"So, you're just going to lay there and listen to music on me?"

"Sure, why not you're saying anything anyway."

"What cha listening to anyway?"

"Oh, nothing just some Janet you definitely weren't around when this came out."

"Oh, what song?"

"Let's Wait Awhile."

Penny lightly tap the side of Dru's head. He had a slick way of showing he was snooping around again.

"I do know that song. I love that song."

"Yes, I have to say. It probably could be played at any era of time, also it's good prevention."

As soon as she had heard the word prevention, she knew she wasn't off the hook, class was still in session, however on what the song was geared for, Dru took it in another direction.

"Prevention for what Mr.?"

"AIDS prevention." Penny laughed.

"AIDS prevention, Dru? Okay, I gotta hear this one."

"It was a flaw song, but it would have been absolutely flawless if the hook would've been used in the background for AIDS commercials and in sex education classes, hell it came out during the AIDS epidemic."

"How in the hell are you able to see things that way." Dru cleared his throat and lit a cigarette.

"Music is probably the biggest tool next to television anywhere you go. Social development, remember?"

"Oh, so we're on assignment, are we?"

"Absolutely Hon. Ain't no fuckin' around. I know your nose is hooked so come on wit the questions." Finally, Penny got her chance to trip Dru up about something.

"If I remember correctly, your last words were shut up and just walk with you, remember?" Dru tilted his head up.

"Did I really say that?"

"Yes, sir. You definitely did. So, I think I should be allowed to ask anything I want."

"Sure, but I might not answer with answers you might want to hear understand?"

"Sure, now tell me about me."

"What about you?"

"Okay, I worded that wrong. Why didn't you reveal yourself to a Black woman? I mean I'm mixed and I still consider myself black, but why didn't you reveal to a full-blooded Black woman?"

Penny had gotten used to how dramatic Dru was along with his sense of humor. Dru raised up quickly looking at Penny as if she had just sat the house on fire.

"Are you serious? She could be an enemy of the state!"

Penny pulled Dru back down she enjoyed being able to smile without him seeing her and plus she felt like her major switched from anthropology to psychiatry.

"Really Dru an enemy of the state? What state?"

"His state of mind." Dru pounded his fist on his forehead.

"Why? I don't get it."

"Because she's the first teacher to the Blackman."

"Okay, I get that but..."

"No matter what state of mind he's in they cannot rise higher than her now would you disagree?"

"Yes, because just cuz you're an assignment studying a few..." Dru cut Penny off again and lit one cigarette and put one behind his ear.

"Sorry again sweetheart. My assignment is to become one in the same with all and right now, a goddamn alien could come to the planet and examine the Black woman in this part of the world, and that alien wouldn't be able to tell if the Black man was on the bottom or the top of the world."

"So why isn't she your assignment?"

"Because she is not the target. Umm, lightbulb Sweetie. I think you need one of those retarded kisses on the forehead."

"You know, you make me sick," Penny said, but now she had to ask the next question and she was afraid because her mother was White.

"Okay then, what about a White woman? It's a lot of them on campus," Penny added, but Dru was too sharp for that.

"Oh, stop it. You added that campus shit, so I wouldn't talk about your momz."

"Yeah, sort of."

"Well first, I'm not concerned with your mom. She's probably a sweet lady, but your momz and popz got together shortly after the Civil Rights movement and among other interracial couples they were trying to show that Blacks and Whites live healthily together. But to answer your question, I can't use her, not in this era in time."

"Why not?"

"Because every mind-state I switch to I find most of the time, she's a honeycomb hideout. I don't know when the mind-state started but I do know it's at full climax these days."

"Wait Dru, slow down, I'm still confused. So, you take the mind-state and become the individual correct?"

"Yes, correct."

"Then if you're living his mind-state and supposedly they don't know any better, how do you know what's really going on? I just don't get it."

"Penny, I and all minor gods on this assignment, we know what's in the heart. I start at the mind and I decode from the heart."

Penny became silent, trying to think clearly and understand all these complex things that she never heard.

"Usually, I only examine her through the dynamics of sex." Penny immediately thought about the White cougar Dru said he had.

"Dru, don't even think about taking me into that sex dimension you had."

"Oh stop, you've been doing fine. You can handle it, but anyway, I remember once I entered this one catz mind-state during sex with a White chick. Wow! Oh, Fuck me Nigger, Fuck me Nigger, over and over again!" Penny covered her mouth; it was almost like blasphemy.

"Oh My God, are you serious?"

"Yes, but the most complex part was that in this particular mind-state, not only was the orgasm met, it was the most passion ever felt."

"Shouldn't it be the opposite?"

"Actually, no. Racism and sex really heavy shit!"

"Okay, so what about me?"

"So, here's the million-dollar answer. Besides the face, you consider yourself Black. You're still half-Black, half-White, you're really in the middle of society."

"That's it?"

"Well, there's more but there's no need to go any further with that subject. So, what else is on your mind?"

"A whole lot, Dru it's not every day you get to go on a dimension tour with an angel, but I guess I better take full advantage, huh?"

"I think you should."

"So how many mind-states are you gonna take me too? I can't really see you having all of them as you put it."

"And you're correct. I'll have to suspend part of my word on that. Basically, I'm assigned to a certain population."

"Okay, I sort of got it, but..."

"No sweetheart, you really don't...it's too early in the flick for you to understand. Those few dimension or mind-states I took you to is for your assignment, but for me I'm looking for an angle, but to get to the point, I'm assigned to a population that is not born yet."

Penny like any woman had intuition and for some reason, she could feel the heaviness of Dru's heart. Whatever this population had to do with Dru's assignment, it wasn't good and for the first time, she reached, and handed Dru a cigarette.

"You wanna talk about it?"

"No worries sit, it'll all come together, I have no choice in the matter babe. But I will tell you this much. I'm on my final quarter."

"What do you mean?"

"I'm at my hundred-year mark, 25 years left." Penny's eyes widened and she pushed Dru off her lap.

"Til what? Tell me!" Penny said in a panic, but Dru sat calmly with a slight smile without emotion.

"Are you sure you can handle this?"

"Yes, Dru, I'm sure! What is it?"

"Well, first take it easy Love. My apprenticeship began around eight years old..."

"What apprenticeship?"

"It's when I entered my body or as you like to put it angel hood began. Shh now listen, minor gods and goddesses are only granted one dream and it's called the Divine Dream of Truth." Penny stopped Dru like an old lady pressing pause on her favorite recorded soaps and ran to pour another cup of tea.

"Okay, I'm back, now you said the Divine Dream of Truth."

"Are you gonna sit cha ass still now?"

"Yes! Yes! I'm sorry."

"Like I was saying, the dream, and I might add, all other dreams, might mean many things but this dream we must know in heart, which was my second quarter around the seventies which you all call this cooling period shit the spiritual realm decided there wasn't any light to be given! That was the third quarter."

"Oh my God, no! What light?"

"There is no more light to be given. And now due to leniency from the spiritual realm, the school of psychiatric chemistry was formed."

"Dru there's no such thing."

"My schooling is different from yours, just like you all have given, all these different names to identify certain points in history; the reconstruction era wasn't in the 20s sweetheart. We are in it now."

"Dru how can you sit so calmly and explain this?"

"Hmm, you might not understand but we don't deal with good and bad, my heart only knows justice."

"So, what does this school do?"

"No, honey it's about what those like myself are going to do."

"And what's that?"

"Diffuse the pathologist. Now guess what?" Penny and Dru's guess what didn't mix and he couldn't stop now.

"No Dru, I hate when you do this."

"Yeah, you got it. No more for today." Penny fell silent for a moment, and pulled Dru back down on her lap, but her curiosity grew.

"Dru, you know you on some real bullshit."

"Now why would you say that?"

"Because you give me a whole lot. Then you just cut it short and besides, we still got the rest of the day, so we're gonna relax, and you're gonna tell me about this Divine Dream of yours."

"Well, since you insist, and it would have been part of our walk anyway, and I didn't expect to do this so soon. But once we're done, don't ask me why, who, when, or where, comprende?" Dru said looking up at Penny.

In his brown eyes she could see hurt and fear and maybe it would give her a bigger clue as to what his assignment was.

"Okay, I'm ready." Dru took Penny's tea and sat it on the coffee table and placed his cigarettes in his pocket.

"Dru, I told you I don't really feel..."

"Shh, you'll be fine. Close your eyes," Dru said closing his eyes.

Penny felt Dru's index finger touch her temple, and within moments it became extremely hot. The humidity was almost unbearable and when she open her eyes, Dru and her were standing in an abandoned store or a building of some sort.

Dru stood staring out the store front window, off into the distance. His hands were behind his back and he stood as if he were waiting for something. Penny looked around the abandoned complex. There was dust everywhere and sweat poured from her forehead, unlike the mysterious cold dimension Dru took her to, the heat she felt took her breath away.

The storefront window was broken out and Dru gave Penny a nod to go look. She didn't know what was creepier, the broken glass that crunched under her shoes or the deserted place she saw before her. She knew she was in a city, abandoned buildings everywhere, and light poles that laid in the middle of the street.

As she looked at the sun, it radiated so much heat, but at the same time was so dim. Her attention was suddenly distracted by small running footsteps. When she turned, she saw a little black boy run past Dru, and stand next to her. Penny looked at Dru and then at the little boy. He was no more than five. The only thing he was wearing were cut off jeans and a pair of tennis shoes. His hair was long and coarse and brown spotted from the dust. The little boy stared out the storefront as if he were waiting for something. Penny gave Dru another glance, he lit a cigarette and stared out the window as if he were waiting on something also. Penny could hear a truck coming, but it was so loud she didn't know from which direction. As the noise got closer and closer, the little boy crouched down as if he were hiding, and when she saw the truck, she saw all the reasons why. Penny covered her mouth and she never imagined tears could instantly fall. She watched as a white dump truck rolled by. It was enormous, there were black letters printed on the side, but she couldn't see them as the dust rolled from underneath the tires. The windows were tinted and inside were naked dead bodies filled to the top. The bodies of Black men.

CHAPTER 25

Part Two

With a light tap to her temple, Penny opened her eyes. She found herself standing in the middle of the living room and Dru sat patiently on the sink in the bathroom. He looked at his watch and flipped the toilet seat up. His mental clock knew exactly how long it would take for Penny to be on her knees, but he wasn't that precise because the vomit didn't quite make it in the toilet. Penny glanced up at Dru. He stared without emotion with his arms folded and his feet dangling.

"You got vomit on my shoe sweetheart. Oh, and by the way, it's good to breath when ya vomit. It comes up a little easier."

Penny stood looking in the mirror, trying to get her mind back together, but her only reaction to Dru was a slap to the face. And to make sure he felt it, another backhand slap to the other side of his face.

"That's it! Get your shit and go, as a matter of fact."

Dru hopped off the sink and leaned against the doorway, watching Penny drag each duffle bag out the door. His head moved as she moved.

"And here don't forget your laptop, now you can get the hell out of my house!"

"I see that was too much for you." But that pissed Penny off even more.

"You think?! You know what you're a sicko, psycho, crazy ass! And you can now find the door please."

Penny stood with arms folded and deep down, she hoped he would resist and stay. It was definitely the case of said words, that weren't meant to be said, and she felt it as Dru slipped his hoody on and slipped a cigarette in his mouth and walked slowly to his bags in the hallway. But he did stop as if he forgot something.

"So, I guess the assignment is off, huh?"

"Yes, and you can go. I'll find someone else."

"Sure, no worries, but I'll leave you with one question, if that's okay with you?"

"Sure, you've got one minute."

"If I'm a sicko, psycho, crazy ass, then is the little boy who had the dream, a sicko, psycho, crazy ass?"

Since is question actually made sense, that only pissed her off even more and a door slammed in his face was the only way she could respond.

CHAPTER 26

The Apology?

Penny pulled her Volkswagen bug in front of her complex. It had been four days since she saw Dru, and she couldn't help but stare at the stairwell that led to his secret quarters. For the past four nights, he was no show for his late-night cigarette.

"Maybe I did overreact a little, God, I never hit anyone in my life," Penny thought to herself.

The longer she stared at the stairwell, the more guilt absorbed in her heart. If she did learn anything from him, it was that the heart told everything. Before she gave her mind the chance to second guess, she made her way to the stairwell.

"I hope he at least accepts my apology I'm not gonna dare ask him to let me finish my assignment."

Penny got to the stairwell and the latch was unlocked, just as before. *"Damn it!"* she thought. She had totally forgotten about the ladder she climbed and the narrow ledge above.

There was a small glow from the vent and by the time she reached the top, an odd feeling came over her, and very odd indeed. When she peeked through the vent, the secret quarters was empty and she was even at a loss for words.

"He's really gone."

Penny quickly hurried back down the ladder and rushed out the basement for fear of getting caught. The next thing was to lose all her pride and call. She didn't know at all how she must've looked like as she rushed in her building but she could feel the eyes of the students in the lounge area of her building.

"I must look like a basket-case. I can't believe he's gone."

It seemed like her elevator took forever and she finally made it to her couch where she curled up waiting for a dial-tone, but a phone service answering machine was definitely what she didn't expect.

"We're sorry but the number you're calling has been disconnected."

"Is he playing a game now? Penny you're such a fuck up. How do you run an angel away?" she thought to herself. She stared at the dark grey clouds for a moment and a call from Tiffany came at the right time.

"So, what's yo malfunction? Why you didn't call me today?" Tiffany said before Penny answered hello.

"What's up sis?"

"Oh, Oh what's the matter with you? Let me guess, Dru problems?"

"Yes, and I screwed everything up. He's gone."

"Damn, what'd you do? It can't be that bad."

Tears began to fall. Tears she couldn't hold in and the more they fell, the more pressure she felt simply because who could she explain her newfound life to?

"Damn girl. I've never heard you sound like this. What did you do?"

"Nothing girl. You wouldn't understand. Trust me."

"And since when have I never understood? Come on now, what happened?"

"Tiff to be honest, if I told you, you'd wanna commit me to the psych ward." As sad as Penny sounded, Tiffany couldn't help but laugh.

"Psych ward girl?"

"Now I'm worried. What the hell have y'all been doing together? I see it definitely ain't sex." Tiffany always had a keen way of switching any bad moment into a little humor.

"No Tiff, definitely no sex but as crazy as it sounds, he took me through experiences I never dreamt of."

"Without sex?!"

"Tiff would you get ya head out of the sewer for a minute. I'm serious."

"Okay, Okay, I'm sorry. So, if you're not gonna tell me what you did, then what about your assignment? What cha gonna do now?"

"Shit I guess I gotta find somebody else, but that might not be too hard." Penny paused because she had to reveal at least a little bit of her experience.

"Tiff I will tell you this much, and I can't tell you everything that happened between me and Dru but always be careful of how you treat people."

"Yeah, totally agree with that. But that's all you gonna tell me?"

"Yeah, for now sis, but I'm a let cha go, I'll see you in the morning dining hall as usual, tell Ebb what up."

As soon as Penny hung up, she rose from the couch and completed her explanation she gave Tiff.

"Well Penny, you knew for a fact. Be careful how you treat people because you never know who's an angel."

CHAPTER 27

I Apologized

Morning arrived and Penny sat in the dining hall. She usually always got there first to grab their usual table before anyone else got it. Penny stared at the slow steam rising from her coffee cup and gave a gentle smile.

"I wonder is he having his nasty ass cup of black coffee right now. Hmm probably so."

It was nine o'clock on the head and Penny watched as students rushed in and out of the dining hall and Tiffany came storming through the door with the same breakfast, she brought Penny and Ebony for years. Bagels and orange juice.

"Hey girl. It's cold as hell out. You okay since last night?"

"Yeah. I'm good, but I don't wanna talk about that. So, what chapter we gonna start at?" Penny knew deep down she still wanted to see if Dru would happen to show.

"Look at her girl," Tiffany said pointing at Ebony. Penny laughed because Ebony always seem to walk as if she was winning a Grammy.

"Hey, what's up? Sorry I'm late," Ebony said.

"Ebb, how in the hell are you wearing them damn leggings in that damn cold?" Tiffany asked.

"Because I can, but anyway, I saw your boy."

"Who?" Penny asked anxiously.

"Calm down, you know, your boy Dru."

"Where? I haven't seen him lately."

"Oh, I saw him about an hour ago, but it was a real trip out."

Penny got nervous and she didn't know what to expect. All she did know was he probably wasn't the same from when Ebony met him the first time.

"What was tripped out?"

"Girl, you know I gotta drive through the west side"

"Right."

"But anyway, I get to a stoplight and I see Dru in one of them African dashikis wit a group of other dudes."

"Oh God, I hope she didn't talk to him," Penny thought shaking her head.

"Are you sure it was him?" Tiffany asked.

"Yeah, I'm sure but they was standing on the corner, talking about the White man, the Devil, and shit. I knew he was Muslim or something."

"Ebb, where was they at?"

"I think I was at Madison and Pulaski."

"Tiff, you got class this afternoon, tell Professor Brooks I was sick, I'll get the notes from you later. I gotta go."

Before Tiffany or Ebony could even respond, Penny had packed her books up and was out the door. The escalator was packed with students and a few polite 'excuse me's' was all Penny could say as she rushed, fumbling through her purse for her car keys and rehearsing apologetic words to Dru, but a sudden eye contact met her at the doorway. She froze as the mysterious guy tapped his cigarette. He was dressed in a suit, mobster style, and he lit his cigarette inside the building as if smoking was allowed. She couldn't help but stare at him puzzled, this time he appeared and Dru wasn't around, but the mysterious guy simply winked his eye, looked at his watch and left. Penny hadn't even realized she was holding her breath the entire time.

"Now what the hell is he doing here?" Penny thought as she exhaled.

She walked outside slowly to see the young man strolling down the sidewalk with his sports jacket thrown over his shoulder, one hand in his pocket and the slyest walk she'd ever seen. Without a doubt, she definitely had to find Dru.

As she got closer and closer to where Ebony said she saw Dru, she had an urge to turn back, still overwhelmed with doubt if he would even accept her apology.

"Now where the hell is, he?" Penny thought pulling her car to the side.

It was still early but on each corner there was no sign of Dru. She sat for a moment and patience as in her favor. For some reason she took a glance in the alley across the street to see Dru squatted down, tearing a bag of garbage open. Regardless of the fact he was in the garbage, she didn't care, and quickly made a U-turn. As she pulled next to him and rolled her window down, Dru spoke before she could.

"Glad you showed, I see you got outta your emotions."

It became old news for her to keep wondering what would come from him next, but she was still amazed that it was like he wasn't bothered by her outburst.

"Dru can we talk?"

"Sure, gimme one sec while I put these bags in you backseat."

"Oh, I know he isn't gonna put that damn trash in my backseat!" And before she could say anything, she had the bags of trash in her backseat and Dru in the front seat.

"Dru! Can you get that trash out my backseat?!"

"Sorry babe, you're the one that found me and besides, I just got off my lunch, I'm back on assignment now you wanted to talk." Penny figured quick that she was stuck with the trash.

"Dru I came to say I'm sorry."

Penny couldn't get mad at the smile Dru had because he did have the upper hand but his response was the usual. She was never ready.

"Sorry? Yeah, I guess you are a sorry Mutha fucker." Penny took a deep swallow and couldn't figure if maybe she deserved that.

"Dru really? I said I'm sorry. That's how you feel?"

"No, I always wanted to say that sweetheart, the correct way to make amends is to say, I apologize. I must say Anita knows best don't ya think?"

"What's with you and music?"

"It's the language of the soul and I'm still waiting so hurry up, we have work to do."

"I apologize Dru, do you accept?"

Dru lit a cigarette and folded his arms looking at the trash bags. Penny waited patiently for him to

answer and she noticed that he wasn't wearing a dashiki. Between the time Ebony saw him, he switched and was wearing a black hoodie, a camo shirt, and Timb boots.

"Hello!" Penny said.

"My bad and yes I accept."

"Dru, why in the hell were you wearing a dashiki earlier, and on the corner with some other guys? Ebony said she saw you."

"Yeah, I saw her raggedy ass when she passed by and the dashiki shit, I was just examining a particular mind-state. You know the routine."

"Yeah, I know and she said she heard y'all calling the white man the devil, you wanna decode that for me cuz I didn't..."

"No worries sweetheart, simple and plain that mind-state totally confused and deep down when I decoded from the heart, I felt that it was too fuckin' cold to be wearing a damn dashiki. It's twenty degrees out, comprende?" Penny laughed because she was finally with Dru again.

"And the Devil part?" Penny asked folding her arms.

"Yeah, Yeah. I know ya momz is White, so what I got from that mind-state was double confusion and deep down inside well, the White man doesn't care about poor Black men standing on the corner calling him a Devil. Now get out this alley. I gotta finish examining this trash."

Penny rolled her eyes because even though five days passed, it was like they never parted and she was back in the midst of Dru's heavenly madness.

CHAPTER 28

Suburban and Ghetto Garbage

Penny pulled her bug to a nearby park and Dru hopped out, dragging the three bags of trash on the ground. Before she could even get into the trash part of the deal, she became distracted by his new look. The camouflage definitely was a new twist.

"So, what's with the camo?" Penny asked.

"Oh I had just left another mind-state right before I went and got the trash."

"And?"

"And I always end up on a dead end when I go into those mind-states."

Penny shivered as the wind slapped her face and she stood over Dru as he rumbled through the trash. She only guessed that obviously the weather didn't affect angels.

"Why a dead end?"

"You know, it's really called pro-style revolutionary bullshit."

"Don't you mean pro-revolutionary, Dru?"

"No! You forgot to add the style, you know niggaz wearing camo and deep down inside really ain't prepared for no damn guerrilla warfare."

"But you're still wearing them."

"Yeah, I know I didn't have time to change and besides, they were of better use to dig in the garbage can instead of frontin' and shit like I'm on a war path, get it?"

Disputing was out of the question because everything he said made sense and she wasn't gonna dare tell him how even she was infatuated off Black men wearing camo. Her heart started to feel a little concerned as

Dru pulled cosmetics and hygiene products from the trash.

"Dru, you know if you needed some hygiene you could've just asked or call me."

"There! I knew it was all a bunch a bullshit!" Penny quickly rushed and squatted next to Dru.

"What Dru?"

"Don't cha see?"

"See what?"

"Okay sweetie, here's the deal, in order to show and prove there's no such thing as a lower middle or upper class, at least for Blacks anyway, all you gotta do is visit the trash!"

"The trash, Dru?" Penny said laughing.

"He is fucking nuts," she thought.

"Okay, since this is tickling ya ass to death; yesterday I went to two suburbs, one trash bag from each and a third from the ghetto. I went to the trash cans of Black families."

"Okay, and I still don't get it."

"Here, let me help you out; which bag came from the suburbs and which one came from the ghetto?"

As Penny examined all three bags, she saw what Dru was explaining clearly. She saw Murray's wave grease in two, in all three had Ambi soap, shea butter, and an old Ebony magazines.

"Oh Wow, I see now," Penny said.

"Exactly, all these people still use the same products, so these are all the same people, regardless of income, so take notes doll face for the record, one of the most felonious forms of bullshit is a division of people turned into classes and improvise with some different words."

"Yes, Dru I definitely will."

"Oh, and by the way, is felonious a word?"

Penny stared at Dru and couldn't help but smile and laugh to herself as he examined the cosmetics. He was like a Sherlock Holmes dressed in fatigues.

"Dru I got something to tell you."

"Yeah, I kinda sense that anyway. Come on, I'm done here."

"So, what else is on your mind, love?" Dru asked.

"I saw that young white guy today on campus."

Penny drove and Dru didn't answer right away, instead he just stared out the window. She glanced quickly trying to keep her eye on the road. She noticed he had no expression, but the longer it took him to answer, the more she felt as if she did something wrong.

"Did I do something? I mean I had to tell you."

"So, what happened?"

"Nothing, he just stared at me, turned around and left. You gonna explain him? You said its other doors that lead to him remember?" Penny said with a hesitant voice.

They finally stared at each other and Dru gave her an expression of doubt, and she could feel it.

"Okay, I know what look means I know I had a nervous breakdown and treated you real mean."

"Sure, you did but that left my mind the moment I left your apartment. The look I'm giving you is that our assignments are gonna get deeper."

Penny took a hard swallow because what could've been deeper than what she already experienced?

"So, who is he?"

"He's the maker of all the mind-states I look into."

"So, he's the pathologist?"

"Correct and we're both on assignment."

"What's his?"

"No worries. That's later and besides he's just a distraction for now, it's almost midday and we have to go someplace else." Penny sighed.

"Okay, whatever you say, so what place or mind-state are we going to next?"

"Ah, now that we put him to the side, our next endeavor is the stock exchange." Penny slammed her brakes because that was the last place she would have thought.

"Huh? The stock exchange, Dru?"

"Yeah, I gotta go check on my stock in Arm & Hammer."

"Dru. Is this still you or..."

"Yes babe, it's still me, I always claim the "I" it's like the golden key to make myself one with another mind-state even before I go through a dimensional door. Now drive, I gotta change."

CHAPTER 29

Penny Getting to Know Dru

Penny sat patiently in Dru's motel room which was situated in the heart of the Northside in Roger Park. She could see Loyola University Campus from his window and as bad as she tried to imagine what was at the stock exchange, it was useless. She knew her sight was nothing compared to his unusual insight.

Penny sighed and looked at her watch. Dru had been in the bathroom almost 30 minutes and she became more anxious by the minute. Mostly wondering what Dru would be wearing this time, but to her surprise, he came from the bathroom putting the finishing touches of cologne on.

"Dru you look so nice," Penny said. Dru's plaid button shirt, creased khakis, and causal ¾ Timberland boots calmed her down.

"Thanks for the compliment, I had to tape the sides real fast. So, you ready?"

"Dru you sure I don't need to change?"

"You're fine. Besides, I love the pink Air Max, so are you ready? We gotta make a stop first." Penny's heart pounded.

"Yeah, as long as I don't wanna slap your ass afterwards, deal?"

"No, deal! You just need to tighten ya ass up. Now let's go!"

And off to the stock races they went. Penny looked oddly as the door opened because the dimension didn't change, only this time Dru took her to the elevator.

"So, you can use elevators too?"

"Sure," Dru said as he pressed the first-floor button.

Penny could feel she was in for a treat just off the fact they were already on the first floor. Before the doors opened Dru lightly tapped her.

"Oh, I forgot to tell you the first stop is 10 years ago, you'll get time sick for a little while but no worries."

"Jesus! I could just strangle his ass," Penny thought as the elevator doors opened.

She had never been in the projects but clearly, she was there. Dru pulled her to the stairwell and it was a sight she had never seen, the drug line started from the first floor. She walked slowly behind Dru, gripping his hand as tight as she could. She could feel her blush as people stared at her and as she stared back at them out the corner of her eye. By the time they reached the fifth floor, she had seen every class of people.

"Dru, are we almost there?" Penny whispered.

"Yeah. Just chill baby girl, I got this. One more flight."

"Well, he's definitely in some mind-state. I know this is gonna be good," Penny thought as she tried to catch her breath that was taken away when they got to the seventh floor.

There, she saw four men in black hoodies, jeans, and Air Max. Each one had on a Jason mask to hide their faces. Two sat in chairs with 9mm's on their laps, one man held a stack of money, and one had a Ziplock bag with what Penny saw could've been at least a thousand little pink bags.

"What's good my niggaz?" Dru said.

"Coolin' fam, we at fifteen racks, here go ya ten," one of the men said.

Penny's eyes widened as Dru took the money and headed down the hallway.

"Dru! You deal drugs too!" Penny said as she pulled Dru to the side.

No matter how hard she tried, she always seemed to forget he was in another mind-state.

"Baby get with the program! Now come on, I gotta get this mutha fuckin' bread, ya feel me?" Dru said as he grabbed his crouch and raised his pants, smacking the side of Penny's hips.

She could hardly admit that he turned her on for a moment, and whoever he was, he had a whole lotta clout. Dru dragged Penny to an apartment and did a coded knock, a kick to the bottom of the door and two knocks up top. When the door opened, an older Black man with one arm opened the door with a smile.

"Dru, what's happenin' kiddo? Come on, we cookin' right now."

Penny followed Dru into the cozy apartment and Dru sat her on the couch. No matter what anyone said about the projects being dirty, that was false. Penny looked around and the apartment was spotless. Another older gentleman say next to her and smiled as he held his hand out.

"How are you lil lovely? I'm Tito."

"Hi, I'm Penny."

She looked over at Dru who stood over the stove next to the one arm man and she tried to pretend she didn't see the bags of crack on the table. She noticed whatever mind Dru was in, he was more concerned with the glass pot on the stove more than anything.

"Stretch day shit some more and make sure you straight, you, straight right?" Dru said.

From the drug line to the pot on the stove, Penny had never been in the midst of the consumer market of drugs but the one arm man would soon reveal why Dru took her there as he pulled the pipe out of his pocket.

"Oh Dru, I love ya kiddo, you always look out but I'll tell ya this much" Penny tried to act normal as he lit the pipe and his eyes widened.

It was hypnotic even for her to see how the pearly white smoke flowed through the glass as Dru sat calmly counting money, smiling.

"Now like I was saying, you always look out. Just keep getting da money, be glad ya don't use this shit, it fucks wit cha manhood, brings the bitch out a nigga, ya feel me?" The one arm man said as he took another hit.

Dru looked at Penny, then stared back at the pot. She saw the tutelage being handed down to the youth, the only thing that puzzled her was that it came from the user. The very one who knew how to cook the drug, sell the drug, and at the same time destroy himself with the drug. But the one thing she couldn't help but notice was the dialect of Dru changed. He was fusing the baby-girl was pimp language and the crotch grab was like a pimp-thuggish persona.

"Oh shit, I see it now hmmm. The psychiatric chemistry. It has nothing to do with the elements but the fusing of personalities," Penny said to herself.

She covered her mouth, hiding her smile, as Dru and the one-armed man conversed, and the man rambled and rambled. Dru finally looked at Penny and gave her a "come on, let's go" nod.

"Okay Popz, I gotta jet, take dis money, hold it down. Me and da ol' lady gotta handle some shit," Dru said, giving the older gentleman a hug.

Once they got back in the hallway, Penny grabbed Dru by his shoulder.

"Wait. I see now."

"Oh, so you get it now. But just to make sure, what do you see?"

"I saw the mixture of the personalities."

"That's good. This dimension really drains me," Dru said turning around.

"But wait, one more thing."

"What sweetheart."

"The manhood thing and crack. That part I don't get." As usual Dru took a quick smoke break to explain.

"As I've explained, us minor gods and goddesses don't see things the way others do. He's correct, any drug can tamper with a Black man's manhood, not just crack. He'll never reach maximum development but he's still confused."

"How?"

"Because it took a whole lot of heart to explain out loud what the drug does to his manhood. He doesn't see that yet," but Penny wasn't done yet, "then what's in the heart of the seller since you was counting all that money?"

"Excuse me, but you never saw me sell anything, did you?" Penny became stuck and reflected because all she saw was someone hand him money.

"Yeah, but..."

"But what? What you don't understand is I can have a commodity and never have to touch it, and as far as those kids in the stairwell, well those mind-states aren't that complex, at least for now."

"Why aren't they so complex?"

"They just don't know and their hearts aren't corrupt, that why they don't feel remorse for the most part, but a rare few do, but at the end of the day, crack is a commodity and there is no time for remorse when these kids are on the grind. Now..."

"That's wrong, Dru." Dru lit his cigarette.

"What is the difference between selling fucking apples and crack?"

"A whole lot Dru. Apples don't destroy communities!" Dru smiled and Penny's nostrils flared in anger.

"What's so funny?"

"That's good. Apples don't destroy communities but Penny and this is dangerous the drug dealer hasn't died out obviously. This is the year 2006, nor has bullshit pimpism, but you don't understand what can be bred from it. Those children are going to advance in the most dangerous ways," Dru paused blowing smoke in the air, "so far, I've never given you a heads up but this next dimension will be in the future, around the ending of my assignment, so don't look at it as just the stock exchange, you must see it as honeycomb hideouts and dead end avenues that still won't work. Now can we proceed because this dimension really bugs me up."

"Bugs you up how?"

"Well love, if you got any loose screws, you betta tighten em' up. Let's go!"

CHAPTER 30

The Black Women's Ass

As soon as the elevator doors closed, Penny watch as Dru pressed button eight and the doors opened to an enormous building of business and trade. Men of all types of races, some casually dressed, many in business suits. When she focused back on Dru, it was too late to ask any questions, she could tell from the way he was smiling and rubbing his hands as if he had paws, he had already flipped into another mind-state.

"What are you staring at?"

Penny jumped back as Dru stared at the numbers on the huge monitors and he clinched his fist as if he just struck the lottery, yelling from the top of his lungs, "I GOT B KING SOD! I GOT B KING SOD!"

"Dru what about baking soda?" Penny said in a slight panic because even the people that were staring at the same board, holding champagne glasses yelled and smiled back at Dru, "we got baking soda!"

"Excellent investment sweetie, excellent I must say." Penny looked oddly at Dru because his accent changed but she had no choice but to go with the flow.

"Dru! You still didn't answer my question, why you so excited about baking soda?"

"Ya see boo! Them stupid ass niggaz, talkin' bout they flippin' money sellin' crack, naw baby girl, dis where the mutha fuckin' bread at. Ya feel me?"

For some reason, Penny could sense wickedness in this building and she definitely knew she was not at the mercantile in downtown Chicago when she saw an Asian, an Arab, and a White woman walk pass in string bikinis and high heels.

"Dru! What the hell is that?" Penny said pointing.

"Don't point boo, that's not lady like. Now, like I was saying, the investment is good, come on I'm a show you," Dru said dragging Penny closer to the monitor.

"Dru. I don't know how to read all that shit and why you so geeked up on baking soda?" Dru grabbed his crotch and raised his ants and put his feet in square form.

"Ya see boo, while niggaz thinkin' crack-cocaine flippin' itself back into crack-cocaine I go to the real mirror image."

"Mirror image, Dru???" Penny gave her usual slight smile as Dru dialed switched again.

"Yes, sweetheart, crack cocaine mirror is the baking soda. Crack sales go up which means the main commodity needed to make the drug is a good investment. So, what do I do?" Penny tried to hold her composure because she couldn't believe that here mind was actually merging humorously with what she was hearing.

"Okay Dru, what do you do?"

"Oh, I'll put little change in the crack game and then," Dru's index and middle finger moved like scissors and of course his mind-state switched again, "I cut it! Ya prices too high, you need to cut it! Cut it! Cut it! Get it!"

"Dru you are a hot mess."

But Dru totally ignored her and focused his attention on the three women who walked by in thongs and string bikinis, standing on a small platform. The strange part, prestigious men smoking fat cigars watched as they got their backsides measured.

"Now once I get straight on da capital, I got to invest in dat, ya feel me?"

"Ass, Dru?!"

"Ya got damn right! Ya see all those ass injections. Ya see baby doll, the Black woman ass is the commodity..."

"Yeah, Dru but I don't see no Black woman."

"Who cares! The only thing that matter baby is the Black woman's ass is da commodity." Dru's accent switched again, "therefore lovely, the Black woman's ass produced the mass production of silicone," Dru's accent switched again, "so those White Arab, Chinese, Armenian, and whatever da fuck else race of bitches wit flat asses those fat asses ya see is the mirror image of the black woman's ass, get it?! So, silicone is the best route, ya dig?" But Penny's attention was distracted by a young man who was apparently getting chewed out by an investor.

"Look! I don't give a shit what you have to do! You tell the assholes at the record label that I said I'll pull all my money I put in! The fucking deal was to find a rapper to make a damn hook!"

"Yes sir, but with heroin already on the rise, and it's a nasty drug I..."

"I don't give a shit! I got a mass supply of pharmaceuticals from India and they're on my ass! I better start making some sales!"

Dru lightly poked the back of Penny's shoulder and by his touch she finally could tell when he went back to his angelic form.

"Well, I think we're done here; I need a cup of coffee and you need a cup of cocoa."

As they went through the revolving doors of the building, Penny looked back to see the dimensions change to just an ordinary business building and Dru was off to a nearby vendor to buy their drinks.

"Here, this is a nice bench," Dru said. Penny sipped her cocoa staring at Dru.

"So, do you see pathology mathematics?" Dru asked.

"Yeah, Dru, you could win a damn Oscar. I saw the pimp mind-state, the thuggish shit, and an educated man, am I right?"

"Correct. Many say three can't equal into one. That's absolutely false, a Blackman can be eight maybe even ten different ones at the same time."

"Dru, I kinda saw the part about the drugs, but you think the stock exchange really works off the Black woman's butt?"

"I wouldn't have took you there if it didn't, but I think you're missing the point of the mind-state that's bred it in the 90s."

"What happened in the 90s?" Dru looked off in the distance and lit his cigarette.

"Hmm two-feet those stupid asses."

"What's two-feet? And what stupid asses Dru? You seem upset."

"Well sweetie, there was never a point in history where the Black woman gave a damn about her ass until stupid ass Black men made it a commodity, and Black women knew do they capitalized off it you know music videos, magazines, and shit for a lot of them, paying for school and all that good stuff, and then they hauled ass, get it!" Penny laughed.

"Yeah, it's a whole lotta ass out there these days, but why you say two-feet?"

"Because look what it bred. Hun here, let me show you. Let's say the average height for a woman is five feet."

"Okay."

"Then from her ass down you gotta bout two feet, correct?"

"God, I can't wait to hear this."

"Okay, Dru, that's correct."

"So sweetheart, at the end of the day, if the mind-state of these Black males is only focused on the Black woman's ass, I don't give a damn how much he knows, the Black woman is gonna keep haulin' ass! Movin' up in the world and he will never rise any further than her ass which is two-feet, get it!"

"Dru, if you say do, I get it one more time, I'm a smack yo ass! Get it!"

CHAPTER 31

Ma'at

"You're doing well. Now, remain as you are and test her."

CHAPTER 32

Professor Brooks Lecture

The next day Penny sat in class staring at her watch, while Professor Brooks lecture almost went in one ear and out the other. Her mind was to a world which she never saw, and everything else was elementary. Dru had her to leave class exactly at 10:15 a.m. and a 2016 black BMW would be outside the building. Her leg twitched up and down and the bell finally rang. By the time she raced down the escalator, she was one minute late, but as Dru assured her, a black BMW with tinted windows was parked outside. She noticed the engine was running and she didn't hesitate, she rushed to the passenger door, but it was locked, and the back-door window eased down, where she could only see Dru's face.

"You're a minute late, now hurry, get in."

"Hey! Why aren't you driving? Whose car is this?" Penny said.

"No worries," he went in the store.

"Who is he?" But before Dru could answer, a young Arab got in the car, lit a cigarette and pulled off.

"It's okay, he can't see or hear us stop panicking."

"But you didn't take me through a door."

"I know you're with me, remember? Now we've got one stock exchange event, so enjoy the ride. We've got about thirty minutes back out west with traffic," Dru said as he opened his laptop.

Penny just rolled her eyes but noticed his attire was quite simple, a navy pea coat, creased jeans, and plain black boots with a gleaming tip shine.

"So, who is he?"

"No worries, you'll see. Can you light this cigarette? I'm trying to type."

Penny grabbed his lighter and lit his cigarette which dangled from his mouth. She couldn't help but be nosy and peak at the screen, but what she saw made her grab it and turn it her way. She was amazed to see a periodic table; the only thing was there were no letters just circles with a number in each one.

"What's this Dru?"

"That's the table we use."

"It looks like the periodic table but where are the elements?"

"Our table is different; this is the table of psychiatric chemistry."

Penny stared at the screen and the table began to rearrange itself. Certain numbers began to blend with others.

"Wow! Why is it doing that?"

"You see every circle with a number represents a certain mind-state, the numbers or circles you see fusing is what I demonstrated yesterday. This is what's happening as we speak."

"But what's the point?"

"Okay, just watch." Penny stared at a circle with the number nine blended with a circle with the number twenty and a third circle appeared.

"So, what's that mean?"

"Well, the number mine is a mind-state that drinks lean all day."

"What the hell is lean?"

"Synthetic heroin babe, but somehow, for whatever reason is the gang-bangin' mind-state. Once they merge, you got the birth of circle twenty-nine, understand?"

"So, what's twenty-nine?" Penny asked staring out at the traffic that she could barely see.

"Basically, you got a walking biohazard to society."

"Yeah. Dru, I kinda figured you were gonna say that. So, these are the people you're assigned to also?"

"No, love. I'm assigned to the ones who might by reproduced by these mind-states. Basically, a throwaway population."

Those words made Penny's stomach turn and the car finally got off the expressway. Dru closed his laptop as Penny stared at the young Arab as he drove slowly down a block as if he were looking for something.

"Now what the hell does this have to do with the stock exchange?" Penny thought staring at Dru who sat so calmly.

When the young man pulled over, he let his window down halfway, she could hear the drug sellers running to the car.

"Hey how many I got dat cush! Yo, ova here, I got dat gas!"

Penny leaned forward, watching the young Arab pull out a 20 and got handed a sack of weed. Without a doubt, Penny could smell it through the bag. The man pulled and a made a quick turn and stared at the bag for a moment and threw it out the window.

"Dru, why did he just do that?!"

"Shhh, pay attention, something we very seldom do."

Penny leaned back as the young man went around the same block and pulled into a vacant lot and got on his cell phone. Penny listened closely.

"Ah! How are you my brother?" And then his language switched to a foreign language.

"Dru is that Arabic?"

"No honey, that's Greek sweetheart. This is his vacant lot he just sold to the Greeks." The young man hung up the phone and got out the car. Penny was still in limbo.

"So, what now Dru?"

"Are you hungry? I am. Here follow me out my side, not your side. Come on."

Penny scooted to the other side and Dru grabbed both her hands, helping her out, but the once vacant lot had a greasy food restaurant named, "Fat Joes Pizza."

"Now do you see the deal?"

"Dru and you bet not say "get it" but no, I don't see a stock exchange."

"Sure, you did. Thing is that the brother across the street selling weed (gas) don't see it basically the Blackman makes himself a commodity in the wrong way."

"How?"

"Foreigners will always set up shop wherever the weed spot is. Simply because weed makes you hungry, so a greasy food restaurant ran by foreigners and even some blacks in the hood, they always follow a commodity that these young boys consume. And it's simple as that, and it doesn't take a genius to set it up."

Penny stared at the drug dealers across the street and she still didn't believe that what Dru said was that simple. She hadn't noticed that Dru had crept away and returned with two slices of pizza and two grape sodas. The longer she stared at what Dru called the stock exchange, a thought with Dru's voice saying, "there is no more light to be given" entered her mind.

"Thanks for the pizza," Penny grabbed Dru by the arm, "let's walk and eat, I've seen enough here. Dru what light were you talking about?" Penny asked but regardless of the seriousness of her voice or how heavy her head felt at that moment, the feeling never lasted that long especially with his responses.

Dru didn't answer right away, moving his index finger back and forth as if he was trying to remember something.

"Dru, you gonna answer my question?"

"Sure, I always forget how it went."

"Well, what light?" Dru stopped and did a right-angle turn looking at Penny and began to quote.

"Son of Buford, brotha of Al Betty's my mama, Run is my pal, it's McDaniels not McDonald's hold on I always forget that part but anyway, proud to be Black y'all and that's a fact y'all!" Penny burst apart in laughter and Dru lit a cigarette, turned, and kept walking.

"Dru wait! Wait! Dru, now that's some antique ass shit! That's the light? That's it?"

"Sure, and there were other songs that came at the time and if they hadn't Black males might have been doomed."

"Dru please don't call me green or look at me like a peon but you're telling me just that song was the light?"

"Nope!" Dru paused handing Penny her soda and turned again to look at her.

"Self-destruction! Ya headed for self-destruction!"

"Dru stop, stop you gonna make me start crying," Penny yelled while laughing, "okay, so you're saying rap music?"

"No! Hip Hop was the only light. A culture that picked up the slack for the social development of Black males and it had did and performed what all the others didn't. But besides all that, and besides Black children didn't really get into trouble by being MC's, graffiti artists, playing with turntables, and breakdancing."

"What did it do that other didn't do? What others?"

"Well, Dr. King and Malcolm X, they asses didn't unite and by the time they shook hands too damn late. And Dubois and Booker T, their asses didn't unite, and poor Garvey was stuck in the middle. Hip hop was the final light and that got dismantled."

"But how?"

"Well, sadly the founders and many that paved the way, and they probably didn't think they would have to move in such a way, basically they supposed to LLC, INC, CO, the damn name, but woulda, coulda, shoulda too damn late for that shit, it got stolen."

"You mean the light?"

"No, the name. Pretty much, I could invest in nylon, make some damn G-strings and thongs, and call em hip hop thongs and get away with it and make gold."

"Okay but..."

"But what? There is no but. No matter what the culture or light is, if you steal the name and replace it with nonsense and remember what we said nonsense is..." Penny immediately cut Dru off.

"A deadly weapon. I want you to show me one."

"One what?"

"Take me into a dimension of nonsense, I wanna see." Dru grabbed his wallet.

"Babe, I don't have to do that damn I wish it wasn't so cold, ya ass might get a cold."

"What?"

"Yeah, I'd have you take ya jeans off and give you these hundreds and tell you to throw em' in the air and make it rain. Complete nonsense."

"But that's in videos Dru."

"And you don't see Bill Gates, Oprah, or Donald Trump throwing money in the fuckin' air on TV, only Black men."

Penny locked arms with Dru and the grey clouds covered the sun, even though the temp was dropping, Dru's wisdom distracted her mind from the cold, and she couldn't help but lean her head on Dru's shoulder.

"I see you're enjoying the walk?" Penny giggled.

"Which one? The assignment or this one?"

"Well, I would have to say this one."

"And why is that?"

"Honestly, I like you without all the mind-states, they're a paradox and so contradictory you know?"

"That's good, the population I'm assigned to are very confused. But I sense right now, you're getting ready to get nosy," Dru said as he pulled out a mini carrot cake.

Penny smacked her lips, staring at Dru as he licked the cream off his index finger.

"You not gonna offer? I love carrot cake!"

"And you should know that I know that already."

"So, like I said, you gonna offer?"

"Well, if I give you a piece, then you gonna start beggin'," Dru said.

"Oooh! I don't hate you, but you make me sick and stop laughing."

It wasn't just the carrot cake and the stinginess that came behind it, but the fact that Dru had a sort of Peter Pan syndrome, but he finally gave in and split the carrot cake. Penny ate the cake as fast as she could and Dru stared as she rolled her eyes after every bite.

"What? Yes, I love carrot cake, quit staring at me like that."

"It's good to eat but I suggest you hurry before that carrot cake eats up that thought you had just a moment ago."

"I'm sorry. I mean I apologize, but I wanna know can you do something if I ask?"

"It depends, what is it?" Penny stopped, letting Dru's arm go, and she folder her arms, and she could tell that maybe for once she caught Dru off guard.

"I'm almost afraid to ask."

"I suggest you get it out now while I'm in a good mood."

Penny hesitated and bit the bottom of her lip. Since she was with an angel why not take the most golden opportunity.

"Take me to see God!"

CHAPTER 33

Dru is Questioned by Penny

Dru heard her question and looked up at the sky taking a deep breath and Penny's eyes followed his, she felt anxious and a little bit of joy in the way Dru looked at the sky.

"So, is that a yes?" Penny asked.

"What makes you think it's a yes?"

"Because you're looking up at the Heavens."

"No Sweetie, I was looking at the sky because it looks like it's gonna fuckin' snow," Dru said lighting his cigarette.

'I shoulda known his ass was not gonna make this easy,' Penny thought to herself folding her arms again, giving Dru her fake demanding look.

"Well to answer your question, sure," Dru said calmly.

"Dru are you serious?! I'm serious right now, why'd you grant that so easily?"

"Because you just passed your first exam."

"I didn't know you were gonna give me exams. I'm so honored I don't even know why I passed," Penny said sarcastically.

"You should be honored, hun, you just destroyed one of the most dangerous tools taught to Black males in the social development. Religion wise."

"The most dangerous? I've never destroyed anything in my life."

"Sure, you did. You're not God-fearing. You simply just asked to see God. Very good."

"Dru you might drop me to a B."

"And why is that?"

"Because I'm God fearing and a Christian."

"You might be a Christian, but you're not God fearing, or you wouldn't have asked to go see God."

"Okay Dru, but I just wanted to see Heaven and I guess God," Penny froze in confusion, "shit I don't know what I'm trying to say."

"Actually, you shoulda just went with your first heart, not your first mind in this case."

"Yeah, but people always say go with your first mind."

"Oh please, cut it with ho games. Now how in the hell can I or you go off our first mind when you were taught to fear something you can't see? Umm lightbulb!"

Penny had now boxed herself into a corner and there was no turning back. Her heart skipped a beat as Dru threw his cigarette on the ground smashing it. He stood at attention like a solider with tip shined boots preparing to meet the almighty.

"Now, are you ready to go see God, I have the keys right here," Dru said pulling five huge iron keys from his laptop bag.

"Dru you carry the keys with you?"

"Of course, I have to report to headquarters every once in a while."

"Headquarters? Don't you mean Heaven?"

"No sweetie, headquarters, I usually have to go to get a count."

"Account of what?"

"Yeah, babe God is in debt like a mutha fucka, excuse my language."

"Shit here we go with the stock exchange," Penny thought.

"So, we're not done with the stock exchange? And how in the hell is God in debt? Debt for what?" Penny said frantically watching Dru open his laptop.

"Well, according to the calculations we're about $850,000 in the hole, now come on the door is nearby."

Dru still hadn't changed and pulled Penny along. The huge warehouse was no more than a block away and it only possessed one iron door. Penny watched as Dru placed his ear next to the door and listened for a couple of seconds.

"Noisy as usual," Dru said putting the key in the lock. He turned it slowly and Penny mouth hung slightly. She heard the most obscene language and a noise level that was beyond comprehension. The iron door led her to a top floor gallery. Penny and Dru walked slowly staring over the rail. There were cell bars everywhere.

"Dru! This is jail!"

"No shit," Dru said calmly walking down the gallery. Penny tried to keep her eye on Dru but she couldn't help but to examine the circular building that had over 200 cells. She finally got herself together and found Dru staring in a cell with his laptop out. There were about ten cells she had to past and despite the noise, every cell had new knowledge of some sort, by the time she got to Dru, he quickly shut his laptop.

"Dru, so this is God?"

"Shhh, this is really divine. There's hope."

Penny stared at an older Black man who was about forty talking to another Black man through the wall who was no more than twenty. Each had two enormous books in their hands.

"Dru what are they doing?"

"He's teaching calculus through the walls."

"How in the world can they hear each other?" Dru laughed and lit a cigarette.

"You'd be surprised what man can do in this dimension."

"So, where's God?"

"Wow. You are green. Right here, can't cha see?"

"Quit calling me green. And all I see is a bunch of men behind bars screamin' and yellin', well besides these two."

"No sweetheart, you don't see, but you're getting there. Of course, you see men behind bard but your spiritual eye is green as hell."

"You make me sick sometimes," But Penny slightly screamed as a magazine tied to a string slid past her feet.

"Dru what the hell is that?"

"Wow! Master Jesus' tutelage is still working."

"Dru, Jesus is here?"

"No sweetie, that man is teaching someone how to fish I think he's trying to get a sandwich from the next cell."

After that comment, Penny decided maybe it was time to stop asking so many questions and just listen. But Dru quickly destroyed that thought.

"Penny don't ever stop questioning. It is of great importance that you question at this point the walk is almost done."

"Dru, why is God here this is Hell."

"Sweetie quit foolin' yourself, you didn't ask to go to Heaven or Hell. Remember you said, take you to see God, correct?"

"Yeah but..."

"Penny, the academic, the politicians, the civil right leaders, and preachers, all know there's 850,000 Black men in prison but on a spiritual level, do you understand what that means?"

"No, I don't."

"It means God is dismantled at least for now. People don't ever wanna believe God has to be put back together."

"But Dru, I'm a Christian and this is totally contradictory of what I was taught."

"Then if it'll make you feel better, let's go see contradictions," Dru looked at his watch, "it's yard call."

Dru grabbed another iron key and led Penny to another door which let out to the yard. Penny could feel Dru staring at her facial expressions as they climbed to the top of the bleachers.

"There. This is a good spot now why you look so down?" Penny gave a slight laugh.

"Well, I asked to see God and look what I got."

"Here let me explain, nothing you were taught was bad, the thing is, something can be taught to one group of people and it might help, and the same thing can be taught to another group and they will become dismantled."

"You bet not say get it," Penny said rolling her neck but her attention was quickly drawn to a group of Black men huddled together with one older Blackman in the middle.

"Look Dru, those guys are having church service."

When Penny looked over at Dru, she could tell that she was probably far from the truth. Dru had totally ignored what she said as he looked at the screen of his laptop with a cigarette dangling from his mouth.

"Now what are you looking at?"

"Nothing, I was just checking on something. Oh, and that is not church service. There's a whole lot that you don't see shall we zero in and listen? Dru lightly touched Penny's ear so she could hear exactly what was being said as the older Black man hopped up and down, dripping with sweat.

"Lord Jesus! Oh, I say it again! Lord Jesus! And God said rest on the seventh day! Can I get an Amen! I said, can I get an Amen!"

"Okay Dru. I don't know what you see, but he is doin' too much."

"Well, along with the too much. What you don't see is that he's really a homosexual. He's actually have an orgasm as we speak, that's why he's full of sweat." Penny had promised she would never hit Dru again but she slapped his shoulder lightly without even knowing she did it.

"Dru stop that."

"No, love. You stop that," Dru pointed his index finger, "if you notice, all those boys are in their early 20s and he's about 45, and besides the fact he's a homosexual, he's a religious capitalist. Two sticky ass mind-states combined."

"But how?"

"Simple, he's a homosexual because he's an older broke Black man that is teaching a passive part of the Bible and he only preys on young Black men it's only a matter of time..."

Okay, I don't wanna hear that part but if he's poor, how's he a religious capitalist?"

"Because, for the simple fact, out of the five Black boys, three of them are all momma boys and they most of the time call home to momma, grand-mama, auntie, and tell em' they got off into God. What's more pleasing to hear? So, their female family members send them money. That older Black man knows this all too well. The dangerous thing is the young males already sense he's a predator."

"Okay, then what's so bad about what he said? All he said was God rested on the seventh day."

"Hmmm, my point exactly. None of those men have time to rest, simply because no Black male voice exists for them right now."

Penny didn't want to believe that what Dru was explaining was truth, but the more he explained, and she saw it with her spiritual eye, she still wasn't done.

"Okay, then what about the other older Black guy in the cell?"

"That's different he's teaching one of the primary languages of God which is mathematics not religion. Now, are you done with your interrogation?" Penny looked over at Dru with a sort of stern but curious look as if he were a stranger.

"Dru, you're like a psychiatrist." Dru quickly turned, holding is hand out.

"Then welcome to the spiritual world of psychiatry."

"I still don't know why and how I believe and understand you, and why are you laughing?"

"Because sweetheart, most of the time, we're sent to give an individual a certain message, however if I hadn't displayed a little power, you wouldn't have been able to see anything."

"That's not true you see I'm pretty open-minded."

Just when Penny thought Dru's comical retrospection was over, he stood up, and pointed to the sky and spoke in an old English accent to get his point across.

"And Lo! And Behold! Bring the thunder and lightning bolt! And Zeus rose out of the mighty waters!"

"I like to see you laugh which means you get it."

"Yes, Dru I get it, trust me, I get it," Penny said laughing and Dru's seriousness returned.

"So, while you're laughing, understand that the mind-state dimensions

I took you to are highly dangerous because they live in a world a fiction. Until the mind-states come into reality, if multiplied, the generations with these mind-states 25 years from now are doomed."

"What do you mean doomed?"

"Well, let's go see what happens to some of the mind-states if they do not change, come on, we have to go to medical."

The medical building of the prison was about fifty yards away and as Dru exposed everything of a different sight, she began to notice things she never paid attention to. It was almost as if she had an imaginary lens and Dru was teaching her how to perfect it.

"Dru, now why is he wearing two crosses around his neck? And that guy walking with him, why is he swinging his arm from side to side, holding a belt buckle?"

"The one with the two crosses it's a new mind-state developed, these days the wearing of the cross has turned into a fad, and he thinks something in the sky is winking his eye with a thumbs up as if that's gonna help him get into Heaven. And the other guy," Dru paused, watching the young man stroll by, "he's imagining Black women or groupies are watching his rude swag." Penny stopped and looked around the yard to make sure she heard Dru correctly.

"Dru, I don't see any Black women."

"I know and neither do I, but a woman is always the motivating force in men no matter if she's around or not. So, he's walking with a rude swag as if all the groupie bitches he left on the street are watching and that's why that boy is walking down the court like Kobe. It's really simple shit," Dru said fumbling with the iron keys.

"He's such an arrogant ass. None of this is simple shit,' Penny

thought.

They walked slowly past the congregation and Dru pulled her closer to the circle to listen to the sermon.

"Hallelujah!! Thank you, Jesus! I said you shall not know the hour or the date!" Penny tried to hold her laughter in, staring at one of the boys who had his mouth covered, holding his own laughter in.

"Go ahead, you're allowed to laugh, no one can see us anyway."

"Dru, I'm sorry but this guy is hilarious all that damn sweat."

"Shall we cover nonsense again?"

"Sure Dru," Penny said laughing.

"Well, what he just said is deadly. No wonder why so many of the young are having ball."

"Huh?"

"You can't reach young Black males who live in a damn fantasy mind-state, you should not know the hour or the date, and basically their minds think they can sit around and bullshit all day."

"Yeah, but Dru that scripture is talking about the wrath of God."

"Oh, please, miss me with the games, all spiritualists without the titles know that God can only appear and move through a weak vessel, and you're in the very chamber of where he's at, now we're late for medical."

CHAPTER 34

Mr. Engles

Dru opened the next door which led to a hospital. It was ordinary and all that was really there were inmates waiting to see the nurse.

"So that's it for God?"

"Yeah, pretty much, but I was just granting your wish, but this part of the walk is very important." Dru handed Penny a piece of gum as he came to an office door that read psychiatrist.

"Come on, we're just in time," Dru said opening the door.

"In time for what?"

"Oh, this mind-state is called voluntary mental illness."

"Umm, Dru don't you mean involuntary mental illness, if there's such a thing."

"No, I know exactly what I said, now shhh."

"Why do I have to shhh, you said they can't see us."

"I know, you might miss something."

Dru pulled Penny in the corner of the office, there was a Black male inmate about 50-years-old, being evaluated by a Black female psychiatrist. Dru left Penny in the corner to observe by herself. He handed her his laptop and moved so swiftly before she could say anything. He hopped on the end of the psychiatrist's desk and he sat dangling his tip shined boots with his hands folded, staring at the older gentleman.

"So, Mr. Engles, tell me what's going on?" The psych asked.

"Same thing I keep hearing voices," Mr. Engles replied, clinching his jaws.

Penny couldn't help but to leave the corner and stand next to Dru. She herself had taken psych courses and could tell by Mr. Engles facial expressions and his answers there was something very odd about his demeanor.

"So, would you like to hear what the psych is thinking?" Dru asked, smiling at Penny.

"You can do that too?"

"Sure, watch."

As before, Dru lightly touched Penny's left temple and she had caught the last few words of self-talk that the psych was thinking.

"This nigga so full of shit. Since he wanna play, I'm a give his ass some shit for real." Penny covered her mouth in astonishment because the psych had such a concerning face.

"Well, it's time to go," Dru said, hopping off the desk.

"Dru wait, you can't stop that?"

"No sweetie and serves him right. You know the same, be careful what you ask for."

"But Dru, that man is mentally ill! What's she gonna give him?"

"Oh. She's gonna put his ass on some Thorazine trust me he'll be straight. Besides, it was part of his plan."

"What plan?" Dru grabbed his laptop, opened it, and plugged the earbuds in and put one in Penny's ear.

"Here, I'll let you listen, I have his word recorded from a week ago."

"Really Dru. Your laptop can do that?"

"Absolutely sweetie, the spiritual world records everything. I can't be in three and four spots at the same time, but as you've learned someone can have three to four mind-states at the same time. So, let's listen to Mr. Engles while he was in his cell."

Man look my nigga. I'm a build my file up, all you got to do is tell da bitch you hear voices, then the bitch gone put you on da meds. Boom just know when they gon' take your blood and take that shit for a week so it's in ya system. Trust me, you gon' get the check, they might deny you for a year but fuck it, you gon' get all da back pay.

Penny stared at the floor, shaking her head. She had never heard such nonsense. She didn't know what was worse, the psych doc giving him the meds clearly knowing Mr. Engels wasn't crazy or Mr. Engles voluntarily claiming he's crazy.

"Dru, I'm almost scared to ask what do you do with that mind-state?"

"Honestly, Penny, that's not my call, if you wanna know what's really wrong with him, he's simply living in fear not on in his mind, but in his heart."

"Yeah but Dru, I am a firm believer that he can recover."

"And I am a firm knower that that is truth, however by the time Mr. Engles recovers, if he does, he has already transmitted that bullshit to that young, misguided Black male who's his cellmate and guess how old he is?"

"How old?"

"Nineteen. So, the results are obvious. Now it's time for me to gear you up."

"Gear me up???"

"Yeah you know, it's time to see if you've learned anything and it'll be good for your own assignment you know for school."

"But Dru, I don't get to study?"

"Nope! You don't get to study for our tests, it's either pass or fail."

Penny's heart pounded as she stood in the medical building. She asked to see God. She ended up in prison and now she was the one being tested with no grade scale. Dru snapped his finger to break her out of her daze.

"You there?"

"Yeah, I'm fine but does it have to be right this minute?"

"Absolutely, but first, I gotta go to the washroom to get some confirmation so sit tight." Penny sat down slowly, staring after Dru as he strolled to the bathroom.

"I don't give a damn what nobody says. Maybe there are some crazy ass angels."

CHAPTER 35

Ma'at

"You're doing well. If she fails, you pass. If she passes, you fail!"

CHAPTER 36

The Stability Chamber

"So, you ready?" Dru asked.

Penny could tell by the way Dru was caught up grooming himself, rubbing lotion on his hands and dusting his boots off, she had no choice but to be ready.

"I guess I am you're really not gonna give me a hint or time to study?"

"Sorry babe, get suited and booted, we're gonna take the long way out."

The last door Dru took Penny through led to a long dark hallway. There were cells on each side, and it was probably noisier than when they first entered the God dimension. There were no lights in any of the cells. Her stomach curled because she never imagined such places existed.

"Dru what's this place? Is this the exam?"

"Definitely not, and this is the stability chamber."

"The stability chamber?"

"Oh, my bad, most people call it the hole. It's a stability chamber for the chosen ones. Even Master Jesus had to stay here."

"Stability for what? And I never read that about Jesus."

"This place is to test the mind; solitary confinement is the highest form of martial arts. Some of these men have been here for years and as far as Jesus is concerned most can quote his wisdom, however many do not know the type of disciplines Master Jesus had to go through. But anyway..."

"Fuck God!" an inmate yelled and Penny jumped and held Dru. It was the first time she had ever heard anyone use such language.

"Dru! Oh-my-God, now I don't care what you say. That's blasphemy." Dru laughed as usual.

"Oh please. He's being tested right now. Quit believing all the bullshit you were fed. Remember we decode from the heart. That man you hear yelling still has love in his heart thing is, he's got to clean all the bullshit out his mind. Now we're at the door and it's time."

"But wait," Penny stared back down the hallway, "Dru if this is God where's Heaven?"

"Put it this way. God is dismantled and as long as these men are dismantled there is no Heaven."

"Dru, no! Don't tell me that."

"Oh, why don't you cut it out? Nobody ever wants to believe that God has to be put back together and besides if I did show you Heaven, your little mind wouldn't be able to take it."

"Umm, excuse me, I don't have a little mind."

"Oh, stop it. All you have to do is look at the damn news, all you see is hell. So how in the world can you handle Heaven? Now are you done? The plaza is waiting on us and by the way, you don't need your coat."

"I don't know why he even asks me am I done. His bossy ass always never lets me answer," Penny thought.

Dru opened the last door and they came out the backside of a shopping mall building to an outside plaza. The temperature was beautiful, 80 degrees with a light breeze. Penny looked at Dru oddly and laughed. She noticed he didn't lock the door behind him.

"Umm Dru, aren't you gonna lock that back with your little magical keys?"

"No sweetie, I don't lock prison doors."

"Why not?"

"Because there never locked. Most men in prisons can open the door and leave. But as long as they have the wrong mind-state that's where they'll remain, lifers excluded. Now you're stalling. There's a table right there, let's go!"

The small coffee table sat directly in the middle of the dining area. Penny could tell she was in Chicago from the sight of Willis Tower, but the city had changed tremendously.

"Dru what year is it?"

"I don't know no worries about that. Oh, and by the way, your test has started."

"Right now?!"

"Yes, right now and I suggest you stop talking. People are gonna think you're crazy."

"Why?"

"Oh, I forgot to tell you, they can see you but they can't see me."

"Oh, thanks for telling me."

"You didn't ask. Now all you have to do is observe. You're looking for something. Here, take the cash and order a hot chocolate for yourself. We'll be here awhile."

"Okay, one more thing, why are you invisible this time?"

"Because I have to be for this part of the walk. If I appear everything would go crazy, trust me."

Penny looked around her and this part of the walk would be the most agonizing moment in her life, simply because she didn't know what she was looking for and Dru had become totally silent. Hour after hour passed by and it appeared to be a normal day. There wasn't anything out of the ordinary that she hadn't already seen but she did notice the futuristic look of the cans and since Dru never gave any rules to the exam, her cleverness kicked in.

"I'll fix his ass!" Penny thought as she got up and stormed towards an older man getting in his Lexus.

"Excuse me, sir."

"Yes young lady, may I help you?"

"I was just admiring your car. What year is that?"

"Oh, this is the 2050 Lexus."

Penny couldn't help but turn and look at Dru who sat with his hands behind his head smiling.

"Honey are you okay?" the gentlemen asked trying to figure out what Penny was staring at.

"Oh nothing. Thanks anyway."

"So, did you find out what year it was? I was wondering how long it was gonna take you to ask somebody." People started to stare at Penny.

"Dru can we go? People are looking at me like I'm crazy."

Dru stared at his watch to see three hours had passes and he decided to end the exam. Since her car was still parked in front of his motel, he randomly chose a door and back trucked to his place. Penny say patiently on the end of Dru's bed and gave him a severe but compassionate look. His silence was killing her.

"Dru! So, did I pass?"

"Aren't you concerned why you were in the future? I'm surprised you didn't ask."

"A little but did I pass or not?" Penny already began to wipe a tear from her face as Dru shook his head.

"Well, sweetheart, first I still have to be fair. What did you miss? I'll give you a couple of seconds."

After a few seconds of silence, he said in a gentle voice, "Penny you're taking too long. Just say I don't know."

"Okay Dru, god! I don't know!"

"Well, you did fail but fortunately for me, I passed."

"Dru I've never failed anything in my life. Why did I fail?" Dru went and sat in a chair that sat in the corner and lit a cigarette.

"Sweetheart, I constructed the environment and everything you saw around you. I could've took you to the hood, but that would've been too easy or even the suburbs or even a rural area. Instead, I put you in a heavily populated area, very diverse part of the city, and you didn't notice."

"Notice what?" Penny's heart pounded.

"Penny you were not even aware that you didn't see not one single Black man anywhere in sight." Penny put her feelings to the side and she couldn't argue because he was absolutely right.

"Dru then why do you pass? What are you getting at?"

"I can't tell you everything yet, but I think you should get some rest. You stay here tonight and by the way, we all fail our first test."

Penny definitely missed the 'we' part. She was too intrigued that he invited her to stay the night. "Dru you sure you want me to stay? I don't wanna be a bother."

"No, you're good. And besides this is a special night for you."

CHAPTER 37

1:44 a.m.

Penny awakened to see Dru sitting beside her. She had been neatly tucked in and the aroma of black coffee was all she could smell.

"Well good morning."

"Dru, what time is it? I don't even remember when I fell asleep." Dru looked at his watch.

"It's actually a quarter to two. So how was your dream?"

Penny sat up because she knew she had one but of course, it was one of those dreams that came and went.

"I don't know, I mean I know I did but it's gone now. Why?" Dru lit his cigarette and handed his cup to Penny.

"Well, no worries, trust me, it'll come back."

"Dru now you know I'm not gonna drink that nasty ass coffee!" Dru laughed.

"Why are you up so late reading the Bible?" Dru took his index finger and lightly slide it from Penny's elbow to the tip of her middle finger.

"Now what are you doing?"

"Oh, just checking some measurements and to answer your other question, Verse 23:17."

"What Book if you don't mind me asking? And why you measure my arm? And take this nasty ass coffee."

"Well, I can't hold your hand all the time, you find which Book and you'll know. And minor gods and angels, as you like to call us. We don't measure ass and tits and your waistline." Penny couldn't help but laugh. "But if it'll make you feel any better, you have beautiful perfect cubits."

"Oh, why thank you. I'm so flattered I have beautiful cubits, whatever the hell cubits are." Penny cocked her heard to see that the clock hadn't changed.

"Dru, you need a new clock, it's past 1:44 a.m."

"Well, at least you're starting to pay attention, but now I'm going to explain why you failed the assignment."

"Okay, why?"

"Penny the world is moving so fast and made to move in such a way that the very ones who seriously need to pay attention never see external things around them. They are moving so fast they can't tell truth from falsehood and that's why you didn't notice any Black man in the environment. Get it!" Penny raised up and gave Dru a punch to his shoulder.

"I hate when you say, "get it." Yes, I get it."

"Are you sure?" Dru said giving Penny an odd look.

"Well, since you asked like that, I don't know yet."

"Then let's recap, there are certain mind-states we're not concerned with and there are mind-states that I showed you that will never survive in the future. There's no room for a Black male child born in 2016 carrying the mind of a pimp, a thug, a wannabe white collar criminal or hide in pussy mentality, excuse my language. Those mind-states must be destroyed and trust there are many, many, more."

"No, but Dru you said that you'll decode from the heart."

"Yes, we do, however and this is prophecy from the ancestors, it's crunch time." Penny put her head down in total confusion.

"Dru, this is too sticky for me. You took me to prison and you said that was God."

"Yes, I did, and it is, however certain formulas have to change, some have to be replaced with new ones."

"Dru it sounds like you're contradicting everything, you're confusing me."

"And that's good, there's a huge contradiction to the concept of God. On one end, the very ones as I've shown you, are the very ones to show and prove the lamb and on the other end, their fate rests in their own hands."

"Dru I don't mean to shift but all of this is about race?"

"Umm duh! Lightbulb sweetie, clearly," Dru said humorously.

"Dru, you said a little while back I was in the middle of society..."

"Yes, after 76' when I brought my report to be reviewed, we came to the conclusion."

"What conclusion?"

"To put it simple, there are too many idiots in the white camp and there entirely too many idiots in the black camp. It's been a 139 years since we've had to give tutelage to a mixed breed. As you can see those many angles in this walk." He clapped his hands suddenly.

"Okay, pick up the pace! It's 8:00 a.m. and you got class."

Penny jumped from the bed and rushed to the window moving the curtain to see the sun was up and the early rush of Loyola students.

"Dru! You knew it was eight the whole time?!"

"Sure, you're the one that said the clock was broke, remember?"

Regardless of the conversation they had just had, Dru laid back on the bed with his hands behind his head, holding his laughter in, watching Penny scramble with her hair, and do typical stuff all women did. Every few moments, she would look back and roll her eyes in fake disgust as if she were really mad, but up to this point, there was nothing he could possibly do to make her mad.

"Slow down hun, you're not gonna be late."

"Dru, I gotta get home, take a shower and Professor Brooks can be a real jerk when you're late. Thanks to you, and what the hell are you gonna do today?"

"Oh, a little of this and little of that but I'll be down at the college after your class. How about that?"

"Fine. But don't bring any trash with you, deal?"

"No, here's the deal. Let the door shut and while you're daydreaming and listening to your professor babble, make sure you look up the Chapter and the Verse, deal?"

"Yeah, but you not gonna tell the book?" Dru took his two fingers, kissed, then blew.

"Nope, the message is for you. Now if you keep fuckin' around playin' in ya ass, you will be late, now go. I'll see you later."

CHAPTER 38

What Book, Chapter and Verse?

As Dru said, Penny was 45 minutes late and all eyes were on her as she tried to tip toe to her seat. Surprisingly, Professor Brooks didn't stop his lecture due to her tardiness. After about 15 minutes, she had to follow Dru's instructions. She didn't have a Bible on hand, but thanks to smartphones, she simply typed in Chapter 23, Verse 117 and only that Chapter and Verse from each Book pulled up. Not knowing what she is looking for, she finally came to a word that made her heart pound and she heard Dru's voice, "beautiful, perfect cubits."

She put her head down, not because of what she found, but because she was caught on her phone and she was black under the spotlight.

"Excuse me, Ms. Hampton, since you're on your phone, would you like to inform the class on some of the research you've obtained thus far?"

'Shit! Here we go again!'

"Umm, can you repeat the question, sir?"

"Yes, share some of your research you've obtained thus far."

Penny cleared her throat. She wasn't too worried about what she would say, she knew Dru covered her the last time, maybe he would this time too.

"Well sir, up to this point, the individual I'm studying has mind-states that are purposely made by the environment."

"Mind-states? What type of mind-state?"

"Well sir, I'll explain those in my final report, however the Black man, no matter what his mind-state is doing, nothing more than resisting. Sir."

"Oh! So, are we getting into the realms of superiority and inferiority complexes?"

"No sir, and I choose not to use that language, Sir."

Professor Brooks gave Penny a peculiar look, rubbing his beard. He could tell that there no way she had rehearsed anything she said, but he did notice that the class paid more attention to Penny's words than his own lecture.

"Is there a reason you choose not to? Please explain."

"Well sir, with no disrespect to whites in this lecture, those words you used is a bunch of European psychobabble, sir."

"Shit, I can't believe I just said that. Dru if you're there, I'm gonna kill you."

"Then explain further, Ms. Hampton since the class is so interested."

"Well sir, clearly, if the Black man wears his shoes untied as a style or tilts his cap to the left or to the right, or even sags his pants, these things have come about because he's trying not to become White, Sir. For many of them, I might add."

Professor Brooks stared at his watch, and he could tell by the whispers in the class it would be a good time to end the lecture.

"Okay, that was interesting. Class is over and I'll see you all next session, you all may go and Penny I'd like to speak to you momentarily."

Professor Brooks sat on the end of his desk, waiting for every student to leave and he left his desk and sat at a student's desk next to Penny. It was a moment where teacher became student again.

"So, Penny I've seen you've been at work, good job."

"Yes, sir," Penny replied nervously.

"Did you know simplicity is genius? The way you heled your position was simple and you made sense to the class. That's what I'm concerned with. But remember you know I don't give out 's so you've got more work to do."

"So, you agreed? Professor Brooks!"

"Of course, I did honey, the thing is, I'd lose my job if I said in front of the class, and you're 100% correct. You might be first student."

"Thank you, Professor."

CHAPTER 39

Penny Meets Sabien

Penny headed down the escalator shaking her head to see Dru. He was wearing the same navy pea coat and creased jeans with his boots tip shined.

"So, how was class?" Penny had to give him a soft punch to his shoulder.

"I don't know, you did all the talking, and I found the Book in the Bible with the Verse."

"Oh, you did, I see you took it well."

"And she sure did."

Penny sighed and turned to see the young White gentleman that mysteriously popped up from time to time. Dru did a right-angle turn.

Penny could tell by Dru's stern facial expression, his words, "he'll show manifested."

Penny saw a small man with glasses, a tight fitted black sweater, black business slacks, and black suede dress shoes. His cheeks were rosy-red and he stood with a devious smirk on his face.

"So, we meet again, aren't you going to introduce me?" Dru still held the same expression, she just stared at the young man as he tapped a clove cigarette.

"Oh, fine Dru. You're such a sour puss. I'll introduce myself. I'm Sabien and I believe you're Penny. Wow Dru, she's a winner but guess what, I have two just like her. My finest engineers."

Penny tried to pay attention to Dru and this mysterious man at the same time but she could tell Dru's silence brought anxiety in Sabien. But now she would hear the most wicked language known to man.

"You know Dru, you can't win," Sabien lit his clove and continues, "but what baffles me is you're still dickin' around trying to save a throw-away population. Yes, Penny I know you've joined his camp, it won't do any good." Dru finally changed his position and folded his arms and exhaled. And she saw that he had power that Dru never displayed.

"I think we should change spots."

Sabien snapped his fingers and the three of them wore on the West Side of Chicago standing in the middle of the street. The young man stared at Penny with his glasses on the tip of his nose and she had no idea where the line of powder came from on his cigarette box.

"Would ya like a toot? How about you Dru?"

"No, thank you sir."

"Ooh feisty, little thing aren't you. Dru you trained her well. You know I don't care if you ignore me. Oh yeah Penny it's me and Dru's hundred-year anniversary and I'm not fucking going anywhere!" The more Dru stared at him, the more obnoxious Sabien became.

"Fine, you don't want to respond huh, well just to remind you I'm still here. Oh Penny, he hasn't shown you everything." Suddenly his entire persona switched.

"Oh God. You know my latest engineering project is coming along so good, I've learned to make your whole fucking environment circular. Yes!"

At that moment he snapped his fingers and the world around them move circular.

"Yes, circular dimensions! There black boys will be stuck in time, oh wait, oh wait now this is a killer, I've even invented the latest form of sterilization."

Penny's mouth dropped as Sabien grabbed his crotch and spun around as if he was Michael Jackson.

"As I was saying, police officers kill Black males and now," Sabien laughed, "get this, this Black woman doesn't even want to have children. Oh, what a tragedy." The more Dru ignored him, the more obnoxious he became. He began to jump up and down like a boxer punching the air.

"Come on Dru, when's the showdown? Ha! Ha! Ha! What are you gonna do? Oh, let me guess, you gonna get some niggers with attitudes. Oops, my friend, that didn't work."

Penny almost caught a headache watching the outside world move circular and the people were of course totally unaware of it. She couldn't help but lock arms with Dru and when she took a quick glance at Dru, his pupils had become jet black and he glowed slightly.

"Now Dru stop that, don't get mad because I stole your language. Hilarious you revealed yourself to a fucking anthropologist. Who cares, I have your language. Mathematics, atoms, and I control nuclear fucking fusion! Oh, you and I know these things and fucking gang bangers don't stand a chance. Come on Dru, join my camp." Penny couldn't help but to interrupt Sabien in his drama.

"You're a racist, aren't you?" But that didn't faze Sabien as he pounded his fist on his heart as if he'd been shot.

"Oh Penny, don't say that people call me racist, oh some people call me the Devil." Sabien face switched to an Arab, then an Asian, then a Hispanic simultaneously.

"Some people call me racial injustice. Oh well, I don't care but here's the kicker. Now get this, I got my engineers to construct something called color blindness, half breeds like yourself are excellent at it! And now I've even got it where racism is a fucking commodity. I love it! Everybody's happy off the Black man's fate TICK TOCK, TICK TOCK Dru there's a showdown coming, you know it and I know it."

For some reason, the sun stood directly behind Dru. And after all that had been said, it all was clear. She saw the value of God.

"Well, Dru, just to let you know gold is skyrocketing! Yes Penny, we have a stock exchange too. Dru I'm so disappointed in you you just won't stay out the fucking way!" Sabien stared at Dru, neither of them blinked.

"Dru, you know I love God. He's like gold. I heard Black men in prison, what's the big fuss He's so valuable to my prison industry. TICK TOCK, TICK TOCK Dru. I'm ready when you're ready. I'll always be ready. Nice to meet you Penny. We'll meet again."

ABOUT THE AUTHOR

David Leonard, a Chicago Native took on the highest title, and that is authorship/recording history in order to give answers, and also to gain answers from his readers.

David Leonard as a youth addictions counselor, who has done inspirational speaking at various high schools in Chicago dealing with drug and gang prevention. He did a portion of his life incarcerated, and the book your reading he wrote during his incarceration. David, during his incarceration had realized that no matter how many titles he had before and during his incarceration, he saw that there is a deeper problem with what he classified as a special population. And that is Black men in North America. Are they a problem or is North America the problem?

9 781954 425057